I0577961

Grasp

SIGNIFICANT BROTHERS #2

E. DAVIES

Copyright © 2017 by E. Davies.

All rights reserved. No part of this publication may be reproduced, distributed or transmitted in any form or by any means, including photocopying, recording, or other electronic or mechanical methods, without the prior written permission of the author, except in the case of brief quotations embodied in critical reviews and certain other noncommercial uses permitted by copyright law.

Publisher's Note: This is a work of fiction. Names, characters, places, and incidents are a product of the author's imagination. Locales and public names are sometimes used for atmospheric purposes. Any resemblance to actual people, living or dead, or to businesses, companies, events, institutions, or locales is completely coincidental.

Grasp / E. Davies. – 1st ed.
ISBN: 978-1-912245-13-0

Grasp

Prologue

BLANE

"What the *fuck* is in your kitchen?"

"A sloth. Sheila. Keep your voice down, you might wake her up. She needs a lot of sleep."

Their shirts were already halfway off. Blane was pressed up against the wall, already fumbling with the button and zipper of Tuck's slacks.

Maybe the first date had gone a little *too* well. They'd had great chemistry, Tucker had laughed about some of his zoo stories, and Blane had conveniently omitted some of the quirkier parts of his job.

Like his turn taking home a baby sloth who needed extra help. He'd gotten Gregory, one of his coworkers who lived nearby, to drop in earlier and sloth-sit. Then he'd peeked in on her when he and Tuck made it home after the date. Around midnight, he'd have to get up and check again.

Sheila was just about old enough to stay on her own now, so he had a couple hours before the next feeding. But that wasn't what he was supposed to be thinking about right now.

Blane had been able to picture Tuck on his arm at the

next staff party, neighborhood barbecue, you name it. If all went well tonight…

"Wanna move to the bedroom?" he offered with a sly smile, hoping to distract Tuck. "I hear there are more comfortable things there. Like beds."

"When there's a nice wall here? I'm light enough you can lift me," Tuck retorted, taking the bait as he ground against Blane, then pulled back. "Which way?"

Blane pulled him toward the bedroom and shut the door, then shoved Tuck playfully toward the bed. "Get over there."

"Yes, *sir*," Tuck responded, smirking. "So, do you always smuggle babies home from your zoo?"

"Only when they need TLC."

"That's…" Tuck trailed off. "Sweet?"

Now that he thought about it, Tucker *had* come off as kind of a stick in the mud. He'd worn a button-down and a tie for a first date. Accountant in an accountancy firm, white picket fence, two-point-five dogs or whatever the hell the American average was. Definitely not shared custody of one baby sloth.

He gulped, then redirected Tuck's attention to their growing hardnesses pressed together through their slacks. "More importantly…"

"Wanna trade? You suck me, I suck you? 69?" Tuck suggested casually.

"69s are so awkward," Blane laughed. "One at a time."

Tuck licked his lips pointedly and squeezed Blane's crotch. "Come on, then."

Blane was RSVPing a firm *yes* to that invitation. He slid up the bed to straddle Tuck's chest as he unfastened his slacks, letting Tuck reach inside to work him out into the open air.

This was feeling less like a trial run for a date and more like a hookup, but hey. Blane was fine with that. He wasn't desperate for a relationship or anything. He took what he could get, when he could get it.

The heat and tightness of Tuck's mouth were wonderfully distracting. He hadn't gotten laid in a little too long, and he knew he wasn't going to last that long. Especially with the skilled way Tuck worked in his limited space to bob his head, swirling his tongue along the sensitive ridges of the head.

God, I hope I can be that good for him.

"God, Tuck. S'good," he approved, gripping the headboard and trying not to push into his mouth too hard.

At last, as the tension worked through his whole body, he couldn't help himself. He pushed once or twice, then gasped Tucker's name as he finished, shuddering.

It was a good orgasm. Not *great*, not memorable, but also not a letdown. Fiftieth percentile on the charts.

Getting Tuck's cock in his own mouth was a treat. He loved making his partner squirm—especially before fucking them, although that was off the table now, because refractory periods were an unfortunate reality of life.

The solid, warm weight of Tuck's cock across his tongue was pleasing. He licked the velvety shaft, teasing the veins and head before swallowing it slowly. Blowjobs were great because it didn't take great skill to get a guy off this way, but it felt good for both parties. And it could be intimate, too, more so than hand jobs and making out like teens.

This time, it wasn't, though. Tuck's eyes were closed as he bit back sounds like he didn't want to be overheard losing control. Blane's interest in him was fading, but he still wanted the guy to feel good. He kept sucking firmly, guiding Tuck's hands to his hair to give him a little more control.

Tuck thrust hard when he was feeling it, his nails digging into the back of Blane's head. "Yeah," he breathed out, still barely audible. "Yeah, that's—oh!" Warm wetness spilled over Blane's tongue and he swallowed automatically, sucking gently now until the other man went soft.

He pushed himself off Tuck and flopped next to him. It felt good between them, but comfortable like friends, not intimate. No spark of more like they'd felt before they came to the bedroom. And it wasn't from bad sex, either. Just one of those missed connections.

"I better get going."

He'd expected it, but it still stung before he brushed away the initial hurt. *The guy's* allowed *to not like me. Jesus.* "Sure," he answered. "Want me to call a cab?"

"Nah, I'll get an Uber." In his haste to get dressed again, Tucker didn't even hit the bathroom on the way out.

Blane got naked and wrapped himself in a robe. He saw Tuck out to the dark car at the curb a couple minutes later. "Okay. Cool. See you," he said, but he didn't phrase it as a question. They both knew it was just a polite phrase.

"Thanks for the fun night," Tuck answered, raising his hand in an awkward wave instead of a good night kiss. It could have been from the Uber driver's presence, but Blane suspected not. Sure enough, his gaze slid over Blane's shoulder toward the kitchen once more before he nodded and strode out the front door.

Blane sighed as he closed the door, then looked toward the kitchen himself.

The noise of the front door had woken Sheila. She was making little noises, probably hungry.

"Hold on, baby. I'm on my way."

Blane shelved his disappointment, which was a familiar

routine by now. Not everyone was suited for romance. Not everyone clicked. He didn't need it right now, anyway. He had a rich, fulfilling career and life. He'd forget Tuck tomorrow. Crazy cat lady? More like crazy sloth guy.

And it wasn't a bad life. He really couldn't complain, could he?

The ache in Blane's chest told him otherwise.

CHAPTER

One

FALCON

Oooh. I like those lines.

Pausing with the chest press bar halfway up, Falcon Harper stared across the gym at the guy in the tight orange t-shirt. He had the most visually interesting workout routine of anyone here. They hadn't yet talked, but they'd exchanged eye contact now and then.

Not that Falcon hoped it would lead to something more. At most, a fumble in the gym showers was all he hoped for. That thought drove him to action again, lifting the bar the rest of the way before letting the weight stack lower with a loud clank.

Who'd have thought that he still wouldn't be dating, more than five years later—going on six… Wait. Seven now? God, time flew! All because of one shitty stupid ex.

He wasn't *opposed* to dating, if the right guy came along. But nobody seemed to. At least, nobody who was interested for more than a night. Nobody who was willing to work for him.

That was probably close enough to sixty seconds rest. He started pushing up again, counting mentally.

His arms were shaking by the time he got to the showers. Sweat trickled down his back and made his t-shirt cling to his abs, but he was too worn out to even glance around the locker room for interest. He could hardly raise his arms to get his shirt off.

That made it a good workout. There was no growth without weakness. He'd learned that when he put the first twenty pounds of muscle on. He got a hell of a lot more attention now than he had when he first started going to the gym, and he didn't want stupid big gains now. He'd look weird with biceps as big as his head.

Just maintaining what he had was fine by him, in every area of life. It was a treadmill, but unlike a real treadmill, life seemed to burn more than a carrot's worth of calories in an hour.

His phone rang when he was in the shower, so he ignored it until he was dressed and out on the street again, walking for his car. He mumbled under his breath at how strange it felt even to pull something out of his pocket after arm day. How the hell was he gonna drive, anyway? With his knees?

Falcon looked at the screen: Mom. *Oh, boy.* He called back. "Hey, Mom. What's up?"

"Darling, where are you? Did you get the email? So, autumn isn't an ideal time, but we'll have to work out…"

"Email? What email? Jesus, I just got out of the gym. Gimme a sec!" he laughed. "Or feel free to fill me in."

"Oh, no. I couldn't break the news! I mean, they *should* have mailed invitations, but…"

"Mom!"

"Your sister's wedding!"

Falcon stopped with his key in the car door. "Huh?" His sister, Rosalina, and her fiancée had been engaged for a year now. Everyone had expected the wedding to be a few years in the future. "That's... *this* autumn?"

"I called them, of course. It sounds like Jenny's grandma is ill. And they want to get married before..."

"Oh, no." Falcon frowned. The girls were hopelessly in love with each other, and so well-suited for each other, and both of their families seemed fully supportive. It actually made him a little jealous in a weird way.

Not least because Rosalina was out to them all, and... well. He wasn't, technically. They all *knew*, but he'd never said it, because he'd never had reason to. Why bother if he didn't have a boyfriend on his arm to introduce to them?

He cleared his throat. "So, uh, autumn. Right. Who's going?"

"I got a copy of the guest list," his mom went on, and he rolled his eyes. Of course she had. "School friends, your aunts and uncles, everyone important. It's going to be a flowery gala."

"Of course it is." Rosalina had been born with the same aesthetic as him, just in a different way. Falcon's artistic appreciation manifested in creation. Painting, however unstable the income, was his career and his passion. Rosalina's aesthetic showed in consumption. Her fashion sense was an expensive habit. The wedding was doubtless going to be expensive. Luckily she and Jenny were a DINK couple.

Dual income, no kids, stable and traditional jobs. Caribbean all-inclusive vacations, a nice starter home, and cocktail parties with fancy business MBAs. He didn't begrudge his sister a nice life, but sometimes... well. Sibling rivalry was a strong impulse to ignore.

"They can afford it, though," his mother said, thinking along the same lines. "Without plans for kids." She sighed. "And you? Any signs of grandbabies I should know about?"

"Mom," Falcon groaned.

"Oh! Your friend, Spencer, will be there. I wonder if he's brought a plus one yet? Such a late bloomer…" She was talking, but he wasn't listening anymore.

She couldn't have known what a shock to the system that was. Falcon may as well sat under a shower cranked to "polar expedition" for five minutes. Even hearing Spencer's name made his spine freeze into a block of ice.

Late bloomer? Hardly.

Three years older than him, Spencer had been a friend of Rosalina's from first year of college when he met then-sixteen-year-old Falcon.

Just when Falcon was realizing in a final, inescapable way that the men's underwear in Rosalina's mail-order catalogs were way hotter than the photos his friends downloaded on the wi-fi at McDonald's. The school network blocked straight porn sites, but not sex ed, not that anyone had thought they needed it at that age. But anything gay? Hell, teen Q&A websites? Blocked with a vengeance. This *was* Tennessee, after all.

It hadn't taken long before he fell hard for the older, sexy Spencer. And Spencer had used him as his secret boy toy for almost two years before ditching him the moment he brought up telling other people about them. Or even, God forbid, living together once Falcon moved out for college.

Dropped like a hot potato.

Seeing Spencer again, all these years later? He wasn't sure he'd be able to stand it. It grated to think about Spencer's constant smug self-satisfaction. He'd been convinced that his dick was the only one Falcon needed. He'd tried to talk Falcon out of the breakup by promising to come out to Falcon's family at some unspecified time in the future, then segueing to persuading him that the sex was greater than it had really been.

"I guess we'll need wedding gifts, right? She hinted that she wouldn't mind something personal from you."

"That's… a painting, right?" He tried to sound normal, like he hadn't just tuned out the last three minutes of his mother talking. "Of what?"

"Well," his mother drew out the syllable. "You know she's always loved meerkats…"

"Yeah. Yeah, that'd be cute," he agreed. Rosalina and Jenny had something of a wild nature theme going on in their living room. A meerkat painting would be easy. He could do a series, too, while he was at the zoo. Animals were a very commercially viable painting subject. "I gotta drive now, Mom. I'll call you back soon about the plans. Once I've read the email."

He dropped his phone into the cup holder and stared across the parking lot at the front of the gym for a minute, trying to let the news sink in.

Spencer, of all people.

H1N1? Is that a thing? Can I get my appendix out that weekend? How do you induce appendicitis, anyway?

No, he wouldn't let Spencer win. He'd show up being all happy and successful and show Spencer what he'd missed out on.

Yeah. That was the key. He ignored the voice itching in the back of his head, telling him that it would help if he *was* any of those things.

He was happy enough. A hell of a lot happier than

Spencer had ever made him. And, hell, maybe he could find a nice guy, come out in a low-key way, and avoid the pressure of them setting him up with nice boys.

Falcon paused, his key in the ignition. What was wrong with his family setting him up with nice boys?

Apparently he couldn't find them on his own. The help might be appreciated.

But I don't know if I deserve a nice boy. Fucking Spencer. His resolve hardened. *I can do this.*

CHAPTER
Two

BLANE

IF ONE MORE TODDLER POUNDED ON EXHIBIT GLASS, WATCHED by a smiling parent, Blane was going to take a fucking paint roller to it. See how people liked it when they couldn't see the animals at all.

But he fixed a smile on his face as he glanced up from the zoo kitchen countertop, watching the security feed for signs of trouble.

He didn't usually help with the large animals, but someone had called in sick—probably a case of the Sunny Skies. They weren't such a big zoo that he could turn up his nose and make Gregory do all the food prep on his own. Now he was getting the meerkats' lunch ready, since it was almost time for the public talk, then mealtime.

"Thanks again for your help," Gregory told him. "I owe you one."

"Nah. Looking in on Sheila for me last weekend was enough. We're even," Blane told him.

Gregory grinned. "So, how'd *that* go?"

"He was all right. Seemed nice enough," Blane told him,

unable to keep the frown from his face as he chopped carrots. He'd also hide mealworms in the exhibit as usual, so the meerkats could forage for them.

"And?"

"He left pretty fast. He, uh, got a glimpse of Sheila and freaked out."

"Come on. Who wouldn't love an adorable baby sloth? And a guy helping hand-rear one?" Gregory scoffed. "He's a loser, then."

Blane couldn't bring himself to defend the guy. "Yeah, probably."

"Okay, off to feed our long-necked friends." Gregory balanced a bowl of pellets on his hip. "You'll do better next time, man."

"Yeah, yeah," Blane answered automatically and waved his knife. He didn't want to mope all over his coworker. "Get out of here."

He brought the meerkats' lunch to the keepers' area beside the exhibit at ten minutes to the hour, and then took a deep breath in and out.

Time for his favorite part of his job: interacting with the animals. Sure, he had to talk to the humans about them, but he couldn't carry any stress or tension into an exhibit, or even near one. Whether they were tiny four-legged animals, giant land mammals, or reptiles, all animals sensed it.

His vet duties came first, but he acted part-time as a keeper, too. There wasn't usually enough work to keep him busy in the clinic all day. No matter what the context, Blane found the most peace in his life when he was working with the animals in his care. Relaxing and keeping calm the moment he was around them was a reflex.

Today was no exception. As he watched the meerkats from the keepers' area, a smile crossed his lips.

How lucky was he? He really did have everything in life he needed.

There was the usual mix of guests: older retired couples, young people having a day off from college, parents with young children. One or two people there on their own, too. He always wondered what their story was.

Blane had his hour-long talk refined to a science. Joke, fact, introduction, another joke, discuss the habitat…

He moved smoothly from subject to subject, and when the time came for him to handle the meerkat, Chilli behaved wonderfully.

It wasn't as exciting as the big cat shows, but he did his best to make it interesting and factual. Meerkats really were a wonderful species. He loved their sociability and personality, even though he claimed not to have favorites.

"Any last questions?"

It seemed like nobody was willing to put a hand up, so he wished them a good day at the zoo and headed to the back of the exhibit to feed them.

Once he'd set the bowls of chopped vegetables in the middle, he backed out, scattering the mealworms across the exhibit as the guests watching made "ew" sounds. Like they'd never seen a mealworm before.

Already, the clever little creatures were seeking them out, using their paws in a remarkably dexterous fashion.

He hummed under his breath and checked off the lunchtime on the schedule on the wall. It was back to the kitchen for food prep—most of the keepers spent more time there every day than in the individual animal exhibits.

Before he left, Blane checked that everyone was eating well today. Chilli had been a little unwell last week, but she seemed to have a healthy appetite now.

Blane pulled open the door, then stopped short and arched an eyebrow. Someone had set up an easel directly in front of the gate.

One of the most gorgeous guys he'd ever seen hurried toward him. "Oh, shit. I didn't know. Sorry."

"Learning to recognize a gate might help you," Blane commented, waiting patiently as the man shuffled the easel to one side. Freaking art students, in the way with all their clutter and… well, clutter.

"I thought it was one of those unused ones. You know, like *no parking here, gate in constant use!*, and then nobody enters or leaves in three years."

He was joking, but Blane tried not to buy in just because he was hot. He could hear kids yelling at the meerkats from over here, and he had to go sort it out now. "Yeah. Just be more careful," he said, his authoritative voice already on.

"Yes, *sir*." Was that a flirtatious wink?

Blane's cheeks flushed but he ignored it and nodded politely at the art student, or whatever he was. Probably a student. Professors liked to send herds of them out to do shitty sketches of animals and realize how much anatomy they didn't know.

Blane politely asked the parents of the screaming kids not to let them scream at full volume and disturb the sensitive animals who lived here. His gaze kept wandering over to the corner where the easel was set up, though.

He was being stupid. The guy was just one more guest. It

didn't matter that the guy had winked at him, or that he had dimples when he smiled. He wasn't going to start picking up guests now. He wasn't that desperate.

But the way he'd sucked his breath in when Blane told him off, his eyes darkening and cheeks flushing…

Okay, maybe there was a bit of flirtation there.

As he wandered back toward the guy, Blane offered, "You'll get a better angle from the other side. They like to hang out in that quadrant after lunchtime," he gestured.

Why the hell was he even telling him this?

It was kind of worth it to watch his cheeks dimple again. "Thanks," the young artist—really, probably about his own age, but built a little thinner since he didn't regularly have to maneuver sedated animals. "And it gets me out of the way, huh?"

"And it gets you out of the way." Blane folded his arms, trying to forget that time was ticking and he had to get to the penguins next. People always loved watching them be fed. "You a student?"

"No." The man laughed, and goddamn him, he was one of those jerks with perfect dimples. "A little old for that, but thanks. I graduated art school five years ago with a degree, debt. and… well… a can-do attitude." He brushed a hand through his wild hair, then played with a few strands of it and tilted his head. "For all that's worth."

"Did that last?"

"Not really. Don't go to art school. I learned more in a year of full-time painting than three years dicking around in class."

"I'll resist the temptation," Blane answered as he started to walk off. "You here all day?"

He didn't even know why he'd asked. *Jesus. Get it together, man.*

That was unmistakably a flirtatious wink. "Yeah. My name's Falcon."

Come on. Get it together. Don't hit on him. "Do you have permission to be?" He spoke a bit more brusquely than he meant to, but it didn't seem to faze the other man at all.

"Uh… do I have what?"

"Permission. I know photographers need it for commercial purposes. I mean, you might be competing with our resident artists." When the guy looked confused, he smiled slightly and added, "The animals."

One of his favorite enrichment programs was the painting program. Some animals like elephants were trained to paint. Unlike certain publicity stunts, they were trained by *positive* reinforcement. Others were given trays of non-toxic paint and paper, and as they ran across, their footprints formed works of art.

A few times a year, they held art auctions for the creations, and they were always a hit with zoo supporters. It was a win all around.

"Huh. I never thought," Falcon frowned. "Guess I better go ask."

Blane nodded. "Yeah. Anyway, the penguins will be upset if I miss their lunchtime…"

"Don't let me keep you." Falcon offered another slow smile that made something go funny in Blane's stomach.

I don't need guys. I don't need to hook up with them and then find out I'm worthless for anything more. I bet that's all he wants, looking at me like that.

Blane turned on his heel and strode for the kitchen, and

completely ignored the impulse to look over his shoulder for one last glimpse of Falcon.

Maybe, if he was still there when he went to take away the empty lunch bowls, he'd talk to him again.

Maybe.

Three

FALCON

"Oh, that's no problem with us. As long as you aren't in the way of any of our zoo staff…"

Falcon tried not to blush as he nodded politely at the poor admin worker he'd just badgered about media passes. "Right. I just wanted to be on the safe side."

"If y'all plan to be here more than once, get yourself a membership, honey. It'll save you a lot of money." Her concern made him beam at her.

"Thank you, ma'am. I will," he promised. "Appreciate it. Have a good day."

The zoo was small, so it didn't take him long to get back to the meerkat exhibit and set up in the spot the hot keeper had pointed out to him. He spent the next couple hours doing sketches of the meerkats.

Falcon's first priority was figuring out how they walked, stood, moved. He could find models online of their anatomy, but nothing was better than actual close observation. Then he could decide what pose to paint—he'd been thinking a family group, if any pups were around, but he couldn't see any right now. Maybe three adults in mischievous poses.

Falcon was staying until the zoo closed. If Mr. Sexy Vet Coat asked, he'd been planning that all along. In reality, he'd only planned to stay the morning.

That man had caught his eye immediately. Sometimes he connected instantly with someone, knew through eye contact that the chemistry was hot. It didn't always mean the sex would be, but usually it was. It also didn't always mean they'd get along outside the bedroom—often enough, that wasn't the case. God knew nobody had really stuck around long enough to find out.

But Falcon was curious anyway. He was going to be here for a while, definitely often enough to get a membership. He might as well see if he could talk to the grumpy but gorgeous vet while he was at it.

First, lunch.

He dug through his backpack for the frozen water bottle, marveling that the core of ice rattling around the inside was still there. On a late August day, Knoxville temperatures could easily soar.

The picnic area was small but easy to find, and Falcon chose a table on the end, away from the kids. More than anyone, they got in his way and obstructed his view while he worked, knocked into his easel, and stared at him. He could kind of see why the vet was so grumpy, if he had to deal with visitors all day.

Just as he finished up his sandwich and carrots, he spotted the guy walking past, toward the red panda exhibit. He had what looked like two plastic tubs stacked on a moving dolly. He was walking with another man, exchanging looks and laughter.

That caught Falcon's eye… and it made his blood a little hot. The guys were clearly coworkers, even wearing the same kind of uniform. But that didn't mean his love interest wasn't dating this other guy.

Jealous? Holy fuck. You don't know his name. Getting way ahead of yourself, Falcon.

He packed up his food and followed at a leisurely pace, finding himself a spot in the observation area of the exhibit.

The pandas were nowhere in sight—presumably kept away from the exhibit so the keepers could do their work. Both of the zookeepers? Vets? Whatever they were, they walked around, stretching a wood and rope bridge between them, then balancing on stepping stools to attach it to two trees. The hot guy put something on the planks of the bridge.

Next, they set out ice blocks around the exhibit, and when Falcon squinted, he caught a glimpse of what looked like fruits inside.

They were joking about something, the sound of their laughter echoing around the empty exhibit as they retreated to the keepers' area.

A minute later, two pandas crept out, looking around already to see what had changed. One jumped onto the tree and scurried up toward the bridge while the other started to nose at the ice blocks.

Falcon almost lost track of his plan to find and flirt with the vet, he was so amused by watching the panda. It was pushing around the ice block, patting it gently like it wanted to break in but wasn't quite sure how.

Then he caught sight of the vet leaning against the public viewing wall, smiling softly as he watched, too.

Falcon hadn't had a good chance to really look at him, so he took his chance now before he approached. He looked so much more relaxed now, not the stressed and easily-annoyed man he'd been just a few hours ago. Interesting.

"You skipped lunch, didn't you?" The other vet walked up to him, seemingly not noticing Falcon staring. "Go take a couple minutes. I can take care of the reptiles, and Annie's checkup. I seriously owe you one."

"Sure, sure. Not like I'll need the favor back, after Tuck," the guy responded in his deep, melodic voice. It was sexy when it wasn't grumpy. Well, it was sexy when it *was* growly, but that was a different kind of sexy, and Falcon tried not to think too hard about it.

The other guy leaned in and said something, then walked off. Perhaps sensing eyes on him, the vet looked around, then caught sight of him and raised a brow.

Falcon shouldered his backpack and easel again, then approached in a slow amble. "You seem happier now."

"Happy animals make happy vets. Talk to me after I vaccinate a bunch of otters later."

Falcon stared. "Seriously? That's adorable."

"They're smelly little brats." The vet was smiling, though. "I'm Blane."

"Falcon. Well, I told you earlier, but…"

"I'm not likely to forget." The vet reached out to shake hands, and his grip made Falcon's skin tingle. The warmth that shot through him wasn't just from the heat of the day.

Falcon had to take a breath as he let go. "Right. Yeah. I know it's a weird name."

"You choose it, or someone else?"

"My parents. My sister's called Rosalina, like nobody else from the twenty-first century." Falcon chuckled ruefully. "At least boys always think it's cool. That's what matters." *And you just outed yourself. Great job.* He turned red.

"Second only to animals, I agree," Blane answered quietly, his gaze flickering back to the pandas. Was that him... coming out, too? Falcon chose to interpret it that way.

"You skipped lunch? To make... fruity ice cubes for pandas?"

"Meh. It happens," Blane shrugged. "Someone called in sick. The pandas don't care. They need environmental stimulation."

"We all do sometimes." Falcon gave Blane a quick up-and-down look, then adjusted the strap of his pack. "I'd better get back to the meerkats."

"Are you painting them today?"

"No, sketching them. I'll be back tomorrow to start that. By the way, I stopped by the admin office and the woman blessed my heart several times before telling me that I don't need a permit."

"Good to know." Blane's lip quirked in a small smile. "So I'll see more of you."

"Hopefully not from the doorway of the staff-only areas," Falcon tried for self-deprecating humor.

It worked. He finally got a laugh—a momentary one, but it was something. "Yeah. Hopefully not. I'll probably be busy with the otters all day. See you tomorrow, maybe," Blane told him.

Falcon was taking that as permission to keep flirting. "See you, I hope," he answered, then turned and strode away, adjusting the easel on his back so Blane had a good view of his ass in his clingy shorts as he walked off.

CHAPTER
Four

BLANE

"Did you get his number?"

Devoid of context, Gregory's question went in one of Blane's ears and out the other. "Did I...?" he repeated, furrowing his brow.

Gregory looked amused as he glanced up from sprinkling calcium powder on raw meat. "The guy who wanted to eat you up."

Oh. Blane's cheeks flushed and he frowned. "You mean, uh… when was that?"

"Don't bullshit me," Gregory laughed. "You know who I mean. I know he's your type. Did he talk to you?"

"Yeah." Blane glanced at the list of feedings to see what was left to prepare. That was it. Damn it, nothing to keep his hands busy. And he'd filled the prescriptions this morning already. "Uh, a bit. He's an artist. Gonna be hanging out here for a bit… doing art."

"An artist doing art, huh? Sounds hot."

"Fuck off," Blane flipped him the bird and grabbed his bowls of chopped veggies.

"Meerkats, huh? I saw him hanging out there a lot today."

"Oh, shut up. I always feed them."

"Mmm." Gregory avoided the carrot chunk that Blane winged at his head. "I'm just saying! You were cute in the run-up to that date with Loser Accountant. Get back on the horse."

Blane eyed him, unsure if that was a sex joke.

Gregory's smirk grew, confirming his suspicion. "And if you end up riding it, well…"

"You're way too comfortable with this for a straight guy," Blane complained and led the way out of the kitchen. "It's weird."

"It's only weird if you make it weird." Gregory snickered. "Besides, maybe you'd be less touchy about everything if you were getting laid more—okay!" he ducked when Blane reached into his bowl again. "I won't ask again. Until we meet again, anyway. That gives you ten minutes to go talk to him."

"If he's at the exhibit."

Gregory broke into a trot and grinned over his shoulder. "Oh, he'll be there. Pining for you."

Blane couldn't make a rude gesture in public, so he restrained himself to a filthy glare and then strode off to do his job.

That was all he'd planned to do, anyway. But when the familiar wooden gates and Plexiglass-lined viewing platform came into view, and a certain man perched on a low rock wall nearby, he almost forgot his resolution.

Falcon was staring off into the distance, his hands wrapped in a way-too-suggestive way around a water bottle in his lap.

Blane reminded himself that was all his own baggage he

was bringing to the moment, but it didn't stop the shiver, or the thoughts of what it would be like to see Falcon gripping...

"Hey, gorgeous." Falcon gave him a saucy grin and rose to his feet. "Having supper with the meerkats?"

"Very funny." Blane adjusted the bowls in his arms. "Last meal of the day. We're closing soon."

"I know."

Now that he thought about it, Blane wondered: had Falcon really been waiting for him? What did that mean about his life? He found himself wanting to know more. "Back in a minute."

The announcement went out over the speakers, and zoo staff spread out to find visitors and inform them that five o'clock was almost here. Blane made sure the meerkats were settled for the night, taking his time so he could compose himself.

He emerged again a few minutes later, his heart lifting when he saw Falcon still waiting there, scrolling through his phone. He'd half-expected him not to be.

"Sorry about that."

Falcon looked startled and tucked his phone in his pocket as he rose. "What? No, it's your job, man. I shouldn't be hitting on you in the workplace anyway."

"Oh, so you admit you're hitting on me?" Despite himself, Blane was flirting. It was irresistible. There was something so... open about him. Big-hearted. Were those the words? He wasn't sure. Falcon's energy was just magnetic, one way or another.

"Sure I do. If I didn't, nothing would ever happen, would it?" Falcon countered. "Unless you prefer the thrill of the chase and none of the catch."

"I… like the catch." Blane's voice was soft, although there were no other guests around. He couldn't remember feeling so interested in somebody before they'd even swapped numbers.

Falcon smiled. "So you're single, or open…?"

"Single." Blane wasn't even pretending to keep this conversation friendly now. "Haven't dated anyone in… a couple years now. Well, I've been *on* dates, but they usually end in disaster or that awkward 'we didn't feel chemistry all night, do we go for a good night kiss' thing, or just… a hookup, and they never call." He took a deep breath. That was a little more than he'd meant to say. "You?"

"Yeah. Yeah, I know what you mean." Falcon glowed again, his gaze intense as he watched Blane. "I haven't had a real relationship since I was a teen, before college."

"Seriously? Shit." Blane frowned. "I mean, if that's not what you want…"

"No. I guess it isn't." Falcon was wandering alongside him to the park entrance. "But like you said, dates just don't tend to do it. I mean, I'm on Grindr as much as the next guy, but if you try and find something more there…"

"You're just setting yourself up for disappointment," Blane agreed. "I mean, now and then it seems like we might click…"

"And then they block you the minute they get out the door?"

"Yes!" Blane laughed, his shoulder bumping into Falcon's. Heat rushed through him, and his fingers curled with the impulse to take Falcon's hand. What the hell was going on? "Did you find out more about the animal painting auctions?"

"Only what you said. This sounds up my alley."

"It's sort of a wine-and-dine night. Sponsors and zoo

members and guests and stuff. Pay for admission, bid on paintings, drink free wine… I get tickets, but I never end up bringing anyone." Shit, Blane was in too deep now. "But, you know, if you're around… I've got that second ticket."

Falcon looked uncertain, but he offered a smile. "That's real kind of you. You wouldn't mind?"

"I'd love to bring you. That's very southern all of a sudden," Blane teased.

They were reaching the gates now, and Falcon seemed to realize it. His face creased in disappointment. "Shit. Yeah, I'd better go and let you go home."

"If you must."

Blane was acutely aware of a couple of the ticket booth attendants watching. "So, see you sometime?"

"I'll be back in a couple days."

"I'm sure I'll see you around then."

"Try online," Falcon winked.

Blane raised a hand in a small wave, and Falcon gave him an awkward wave back and a laugh. As Falcon headed to his car, Blane went to lock up the kitchen and grab his stuff.

He was the last one out, so he shut off the lights. He fiddled with his phone all the way to the parking lot before deciding to do it. As he sat behind the wheel in the nearly-empty lot, he watched the dark screen load, then fill with a grid of small, square photos of men.

There. Less than a mile away, unmistakably Falcon's face. He swallowed and tapped on it.

There wasn't much in his profile. A good photo of him, it looked like he was the same age as Blane, but no profile text or statistics.

It occurred to Blane that Falcon might have set up his profile as bait for him. He'd take it.

Blane tapped out a quick message.

Hey. Got you. :)

By the time he got home, his phone had buzzed again.

You get a prize ;) I'm glad though. I like to leave digital breadcrumbs.

Blane laughed to himself.

So actually, you got me.

He was barely in the door when he got an answer.

Bingo. Wish I could make it to the zoo this weekend, but hoping for Monday. Do you work weekends?

No, Mon-Fri. It's a nice schedule when I don't have work to take home.

When you say work to take home...

Blane winced, then reminded himself that Falcon wasn't that guy. He'd seemed interested in everything going on at the zoo. He paused, then tapped out an answer.

Every now and then we have an animal that needs hand-rearing.

Aww. Rescuing the world, one animal at a time. :) Any fun weekend plans?

Blane let out a sigh of relief, then scolded himself. Just because Falcon hadn't freaked out at that one specific thing didn't mean this was going anywhere. But the more the conversation went on, the more invested he was.

Going to meet some old school friends tomorrow. It's always great to see them.

Awesome. I get dragged to a family wedding planning meeting for my sister. Groan. I'd rather drink paint water.

Blane laughed.

You're not a wedding planner, huh?

I've always doubted I'd ever get married myself, so you know.

Blane caught his breath. It was kind of a relief that Falcon was so open—somehow, spilling his guts about his dating disappointments felt safer. His phone sounded again, drawing his attention back to the conversation.

Anyway I better run. Nice profile, handsome. TTYS? ;)

Thanks haha. Talk soon :)

When Blane came to, he found himself standing in the middle of his living room, grinning at his phone like a dumbass.

He was doing it all over again, wasn't he? Getting attached while the other guy could just walk away. A couple of his exes had called him a hopeless romantic, and it was hard to deny.

"Dumbass," he muttered to himself, but it didn't stop the bounce in his step as he walked to the kitchen.

Maybe a little naivety would eventually pay off.

Five

FALCON

FALCON TRIED TO STOP REREADING BLANE'S GRINDR PROFILE, but like a siren, the profile picture called his thumb to press it again.

Vet in the Knoxville area. Drinks, dinner, coffee, a movie? Let's see if we click and go from there!

(I am not your vet, unless you own an elephant. Please don't ask me why your cat meows so much. Also, get cat toys.)

It was sweet, short, and tantalizing. No other details about him like preferred position…

Sure, he was getting ahead of himself, but the flirtation yesterday was hard to miss.

He really had to get up.

Falcon pushed himself out of bed, leaving the phone there, and rubbed his eyes. One corner of his studio held a small kitchen countertop for coffee. The advantage of living alone, even if the place was tiny and served as both his work and living space, was that he could sleep naked. Morning wood be damned, he could get coffee before he dealt with it.

Falcon couldn't remember his dreams, but he was fairly

sure he'd fallen asleep with thoughts of Blane on his mind. Those sexy, strong arms, the muscles visible even through his uniform shirt; the sweet, wide smile and focused eyes. The growly grumpiness, and how quickly that gave way to a friendly, charming gentleman underneath. The tenderness he showed the animals when he was working around and with them.

Fumbling to put the coffee on, Falcon tried to stop those thoughts. He had a family meeting to go to—his Mom had called it, probably to see how else she could interfere with Rosalina's planning.

Not that anyone meant ill by it, but it was still a lot of fuss and hassle that didn't need to be made. His sister had things under control.

But he couldn't be anxious and excited and checking Grindr every two minutes around them. The last thing he needed was questions about his future... or his past. If they figured out he'd been with Spencer? Ugh. He didn't want any of that shit. The past should stay in the past.

It didn't stop him thinking about Blane as he headed for the bathroom, warmth stirring in his body again. With the hot water streaming over his body and his soapy hand around his thickening cock, he let Blane's quick smile and full lips come to mind again.

All right, all right. Just a quickie.

It didn't escape his notice that, after his shower was done and he'd wrapped himself in his fluffy towel to get dressed, he kept thinking about Blane.

"Shoot me now, please."

"Oh, *don't* be overdramatic, Falcon," his mother told him. She clicked her tongue as she unwound the silk scarf from around her neck and draped it over the back of the chair.

"Says the woman who named us Rosalina and Falcon," he retorted with a grin. "Besides, you know wedding planning isn't my thing. I don't know why you even need me here."

"You have excellent taste. And, my dear, there might be decoration requirements." His mother looked toward Rosalina. "So, your wedding planner: does she have all the work farmed out? We can put our heads together and help save you money."

His sister hesitated, glancing between them. "Well... we're hoping to push up our savings rate. But you have much more important things to do for yourself on your own time."

Falcon nodded slightly. "I can still help. I'm not working 24/7," he told her. "How about setting up on the day?"

"Perfect," his mother approved. "What about invitations? Are they designed?"

"Mom." Rosalina's lips twitched into a smile. "I believe this was supposed to be a *family catch-up*, not a wedding intervention. Jenny and I have it under control."

"Oh, you know Mom." Falcon leaned in to take more mini-cucumber sandwiches. When his mom decided to go fancy, she went all-out. The crusts were even cut off the tiny triangles. "Can't resist."

"You wonder where he gets his artistic inclinations from?" Rosalina agreed, looking at their mother. "It's your fault."

"I don't do art!"

Falcon looked pointedly at the sandwiches, then around at the little backyard. It was the kind of backyard garden you'd expect to see in the pages of a magazine, or an idealistic Instagram feed.

"That's not the same," she insisted, but she was smiling.

"And you gave her the fashion thing," Falcon gestured between them. They were both dressed in bright, floral colors, but neither of them looked tacky. He preferred to stick with simpler, cheaper clothes himself, since paint had that way of getting everywhere. "That's art, too."

"Nonsense," she waved him off.

"Like it or not, Mom, you're an artist in need of an outlet." Rosalina nodded seriously and leaned in, folding her hands. "This is an intervention."

"Mmhmm." Falcon looked at Rosalina. "Pottery? Landscapes?"

Rosalina winked. "I was thinking experimental art. Performance art?"

"Oooh. If we can get Mom to pretend to be a statue on the front lawn…" Falcon hummed.

Their mother pinched both their earlobes, making them yelp and laugh, squirming out of her hold just like they were teens again and had been caught spraying the windows with Super Soakers. "Cheeky monkeys."

"There you are!" Jenny emerged from the house and slid into the wide wicker chair, sharing the seat with Rosalina as she leaned in for a kiss. "What have I missed?"

"Only Mom deciding she wants to do your invitations, I think," Falcon laughed. "Or otherwise desperately needs some outlet for her creative energies."

"Well, I'm sure you could use an assistant," Jenny suggested, grinning.

Their mother clicked her tongue and threw her hands in the air. "Oh, you're as bad as them."

"Why do you think I'm marrying her?" Rosalina smiled at Jenny in that "about to be newlyweds" way that made Falcon roll his eyes.

"I thought it was the great sex."

All three of them stared. "Mom!" Falcon exclaimed while Jenny started laughing and Rosalina turned bright red.

"Ah, not so fun when the tables are turned, is it?"

Falcon groaned. "Tell me why I'm here."

"Something to do with your eye for design. I think she's asking if you got that eye for design from her, or something you haven't told us." Rosalina's eyes twinkled.

It was far from the first time they'd made gay jokes. Hell, since her coming out in high school, the joke had been that he was more gay than she was. None of them knew how true that was.

"You'll have to wait and see," Falcon teased right back.

All the women sat up straighter in the same moment. "Are you bringing a plus-one? Mr. or Ms.?" Rosalina exclaimed. "I told Jenny to make sure there were two invitations printed for you… did you? Shit, did I tell you or did I just plan to? Are they printed yet?"

"We're all sitting right here. You can tell him informally," Mom urged. "Nobody will be checking cards at the door, will they?"

"Mom!" Jenny laughed. "I wasn't planning on checking ID. I probably recognize my brother-in-law."

Hearing Jenny called her Mom seemed to defuse her worries, and she smiled back at Jenny. "All right, honey."

"Whoa," Falcon laughed richly at the commotion he'd caused. "I was joking." The way they seemed totally prepared to accept his news made him relax, though. It didn't feel like *hiding* something. It just wasn't their business.

Yet.

He kind of hoped he'd have cause to tell them soon. For now, he couldn't keep a man more than one night anyway.

"You're *not* bringing a plus-one?" All three of them looked disappointed. It was like a room full of sad puppies.

"We'll see," he deferred the conversation for another day. No need to explain that he was probably going to be sad and single until he found a guy who was interesting *and* kind *and* good in bed.

But it kept turning in his head, now that the idea had been suggested. What a ballsy move that would be, bringing a man to a wedding where his asshole ex was going to show up. That would be a hell of a way to show him he'd moved on.

Man, it wouldn't even have to be his real boyfriend. Spencer would never know otherwise. All they had to do was play it up for the wedding. They could pretend to split up afterward, nobody would be the wiser. And knowing his sister, she'd be over the freaking moon, not feeling upstaged, if he used the opportunity to come out.

It wasn't that bad an idea. Seeking potential dates might open his mind to other opportunities that he'd been subconsciously passing up since… well, since he was a teen. They didn't have to be the perfect match for him, if it was for one day. Just someone he liked enough to want to see for that long.

Falcon just had to find someone who was willing to play along, and he knew who he wanted it to be.

Speaking of setting himself up for disappointment. There was no guarantee Blane would even want to hang out with him outside the park, let alone pretend to be his boyfriend at a family wedding just to piss off an ex. How weird was that for a first date?

It doesn't have to be our first.

He pushed that thought out of his head. He had to wait for Monday and see what happened. There was no point in getting his hopes up now.

It never worked out in the end.

CHAPTER
Six

BLANE

"Where are my brothers?" Roman's booming voice preceded him, as usual. Blane felt bad for the fellow pilots or air traffic controllers who had to deal with that. "Getting drunk without me? Assholes."

He plopped into a chair at their usual bar—not quite a dive, but also not the kind of place classy guys in two-piece suits came.

"Hello to you, too," Blane laughed. Roman didn't always make it to their little gatherings, since he had the most travel of any of their jobs. His airline often sent him to far-flung regions, and he largely seemed to enjoy it.

The rest of them were already there, one of the rare occasions when all of them were present: along with Blane and Roman, there was Dustin, having gotten a rare day off from his forensics job; Josh, who'd driven in from the ranch despite it being tourist season; Tyler, who was between races; and their newest couple.

Nico, who had literally been an astronaut—coolest shit ever—and was now a park ranger after an injury, had found a boyfriend. Not just *any* boyfriend, but Deen Jayse, world-famous rock star.

It had taken them all a little time to adjust to having the guy present when he was almost a household name in music, but he was down-to-earth and genuine when he was around them. He'd won them over immediately.

Most importantly, Nico was so much happier these days with him. And he had good reason to be: they were about to move in together, sort of.

"Tell Roman the news," Blane urged Nico, kicking him under the table.

Nico scowled and kicked him back, then leaned in to hug Roman. "Hey, man. So Deen and me are moving in together, now that his tour is done and he's back living here."

Roman stared. "Holy shit. Awesome. But what about your job?"

"Well. That's the sticky bit," Nico sighed. Deen snickered, making the rest of them crack up and Nico roll his eyes. "Shush, you."

"Can't help it. You give me so much material to work with."

"Oh, God. Someone stop them from flirting again," Blane groaned.

Nico smirked at him. "Shut up, you secret romantic. You love it."

Tyler exaggerated a groan and stood up. "You're all gross. This round's mine," he told them and headed for the bar.

"Anyway, the good news." Deen beamed. "He's gotten his work schedule switched to ten-on, four-off. He'll live with me for the four-off stretches, and up in the park for the ten-on stretches. Barring emergencies, they won't bug him when he's down here. It's part of a transition strategy to get him into another job where he'll do, like… can I talk about it?"

"Too late now," Nico laughed, looping his arm around Deen's shoulder and fiddling with the fabric of his t-shirt.

"Oops." Deen grinned. "Where he'll be an educator. Meanwhile, I'm cutting back on what I let the label tell me to do, so we have at least those four-day stretches."

"That's a lot of fucking," Roman concluded. "Heads-up: my housewarming gift will be a drum of lube."

They were still laughing when Tyler brought back the round.

Blane couldn't stop glancing at Nico and Deen. They touched each other much more today than they had in the couple get-togethers Nico had brought Deen to before.

They were so clearly in love that it almost hurt. He tried to tell himself it wasn't jealousy, but that was bullshit. Nico was right—he *was* romantic, and he was tired of telling himself he wasn't so he could pretend to be okay with the hookups that were all he seemed to be able to find.

As they drained beer and swapped stories, they went around the table to give each other updates on their lives. This had become a wonderful tradition over the last few years, since they'd realized they were all living in Knoxville again, and reunited.

The boys he'd known in high school had turned out to be great men—ambitious, smart, driven in their own careers, which couldn't have been more different from each other.

None of them were straight, and while that was probably the only thing they all had in common, it had been enough in a small high school ten years ago. These days, kids had GSAs in middle school and could Google gay sex to learn how to do it, or gay love to find examples of it. Back then, even so recently… not as much.

Speaking of which…

"So there's this cute guy coming into the zoo sometimes to paint animals there."

All eyes turned to him.

"And?" they prompted him.

"I asked him on a date. Another real date."

"Yes! Get back on the horse."

"That's—that's what Gregory said!" Blane groaned, but laughed. "God."

"That's your coworker, isn't it? Smart man. He's right," Nico grinned cheekily. "Because we're never wrong."

"I wasn't moping around after Loser McAccountant. I mean, he had plenty of warning what I do."

"You have to admit, though," Josh said, trying to keep a straight face, "a sloth in some guy's apartment?"

Blane laughed. "I know. For normal people, that'd be weird. The new guy's an artist, though. A little more used to weird."

"So… unemployed?" Tyler shot at him.

"Fuck off. An artist. I Googled him." Blane felt weirdly defensive considering he didn't even have Falcon's number yet.

Deen stared, disentangling himself from Nico to lean in. "*Before* the first date?"

"He… has an unusual name. And, artist, you know? I was curious."

"Is he big?"

Blane let his smirk grow dirty as he sipped his beer. "I hope so." After the laughter faded, he added, "Not internationally famous or anything, but there are headlines and gallery showings and stuff. He has a portfolio website, and stuff at local art… places. His style is good."

"So a surviving artist, not just struggling." Dustin raised his brow. "Respect. He must be smart."

"He comes off that way. I've asked him to come to the wine and auction for our animal paintings."

"Shit." Roman groaned. "I wanted to go to that, but…"

"They're sending you off that weekend," Blane finished. He was well used to it by now.

Roman sighed. "Sorry. I know. I'm a flake."

"Oh, we get it," Deen assured him. Probably more than anyone else at the table, the newest member of their brother-hood—by not-yet-marriage, if not tacky blood oath under the high school bleachers—understood his dilemma.

"But getting back to this guy…" Roman prompted. "He's hot, right? You're not settling?"

"Hell no, I'm not settling. Fuck you too," Blane flipped him off. "And that's all you'll find out until after we *actually* go on a date." Or even better, until he got the guy's number.

Or at least got him in bed. Because by this point, whatever he said, part of him *was* ready to settle for whatever the hell he could get. Not that he'd ever tell the guys that.

His eyes lingered on Nico and Deen when they leaned into each other, almost unconsciously, as Deen talked about recording some new songs. They'd had a hard road, what with Deen's tour life and Nico being stuck in the depths of a forest, and even they had made it work. And now they had it all, or at least, the most important parts.

I want to have it all, too.

CHAPTER
Seven

FALCON

Waking up to that notification on his phone made Falcon roll his eyes. Then he saw the Grindr profile name responsible for sending it, and his mind changed: *Dates or more?*

That was Blane.

He rolled over in bed and swiped to answer.

Happy Monday. Did you have a good weekend?

It took a few minutes to get an answer.

Can't complain :) Saw friends, cleaned my house. Exciting life. You? How'd the wedding planning go?

Blane had actually paid attention to him? Falcon couldn't remember the last time a guy had made conversation with him, remembered it, and referenced it again later. His smile widened.

Mom tried to take over, I saved my sister, and then she force-fed us little fancy cucumber sandwiches.

I've never had a cucumber sandwich. It sounds very British.

Mom and my sis like fancy parties and stuff. I like to hide in the corner and drink the free wine.

He pushed himself out of bed and headed for the coffee machine. By the time he put the pot on, he had an answer.

Sensible strategy. Coming to the zoo today?

I was gonna stay home and sketch, then come tomorrow. Hard decision if that's an invitation though. ;)

What about my other invitation?

Falcon tilted his head, his coffee mug in one hand and phone in the other as he leaned on the little kitchen counter that stretched along one wall of his apartment. It was the tidiest spot in the place. He didn't dare walk among his art supplies until he was fully awake.

What invitation is that?

The auction... with free wine.

Falcon hesitated, tapping his phone on his lips. He nearly drank the corner of his phone, then put it down to pick up his mug. Jesus, he needed caffeine to think about that.

Finally, he settled on, *I didn't realize that was a serious invitation.*

It was a date, if you want.

Falcon's heart raced. *Yes. When is it?*

Saturday, 6 to 8. But I hope I'll see you again before then?

Oh yes. I hope so, too. Falcon licked his lips, processing the weird shiver of adrenaline that coursed through him.

He told himself it wasn't nerves, but even as he tried, he knew it wasn't true. Goddamn. Why did he let men get to him, worm their way into that vulnerable part of his heart, only to—inevitably, invariably—break it off, or drift away? Neither felt better than the other.

Falcon wasn't just awake now, he was wide awake and restless. Anxious energy made him fidget with his coffee cup, turning it around and around in his hands as he sipped.

He wandered back and forth beside the countertop,

eyeing the half-finished canvas he'd been putting off getting back to. Art supplies were expensive—thirty-inch canvas squares especially. He couldn't just let it gather dust.

It was an energetic piece—a somewhat abstracted form of an animal, hardly recognizable as more than shapes of color, but hopefully with the burning energy of a lioness on the hunt. He'd painted the first layer in broad, fast strokes. Now he was going to add highlights and shadows.

Falcon shrugged on shorts and a t-shirt, his mind already caught up in planning today's work. He'd been planning to do more computer art for his online print shop—one of those print-on-demand places that did graphic prints, t-shirts, mugs, stickers, and so on.

He had another artist persona of sorts online, starting from a blog he'd run years ago. He'd eventually almost stopped blogging, but people had continued to share and buy the cutesy cartoon style. It paid some of the bills, while his painting did the rest.

Until he had to replace his tablet or pen, the overhead costs were lower, and he could screw around with different styles a lot more easily. Now that he'd developed a style he was known for, it was much quicker than his experimental painting.

And honestly, it felt *good* to spend an afternoon doodling personified daisies saying motivational slogans.

One of them came to mind and made Falcon smile.

It's hard to be patient, but you'll bloom too!

Yeah, it was hard to be patient when he had a new potential *something* developing with anyone. Blane seemed so nice and caring, but so many guys did at first before turning out to be unwilling to give their heart to anyone, however gently he tried to treat it.

Maybe the answer was to take it slower, emotionally. But every time he tried, he wound up accidentally blurting out some sincere expression of his feelings, and then… the fade-out would begin.

Could he try it again? With Blane? The man clearly had walls, but was reaching out a hand of—friendship? Romantic interest? Sexual interest? Whatever it was, Falcon wanted it.

The emotions came easily to him as he worked: the huntress, caught mid-leap, dusky orange brown between dashes of green and the blockier reds of her body. The desperation to feed herself, her young, her mate. The skill and finesse. The raw, charged energies of love, sex, and death had much in common for the artist.

Falcon's phone went off sometime before lunch, breaking the reverie of a couple hours' work. The name made him smile: Oscar.

He hastily wiped his hands before answering on speaker-phone, leaving it on the countertop.

"Hey," he greeted his best friend—only real close friend, if he were honest with himself.

Oscar sounded tired. "Hey, darling. What's up?"

They'd met and instantly clicked as friends when they first met at some fancy art shindig out here. Falcon had gone solo and Oscar's date had taken him, but Oscar had wound up ditching the guy and hanging out with Falcon all night.

"Oof. I woke up and started painting. I don't even know what day it is," Falcon joked. "You? Where are you this week?"

"San Diego."

"Jeez. Your feet still attached?"

"I think so." Oscar's dance company toured a lot, which was great for his career but not for his health. Falcon worried about him a little more than he seemed to worry about himself. "I'll get back to you on that. So what's the latest?"

"My sister's wedding," Falcon groaned. "Mom's trying to take charge. They want me to go help set up and whatever, which I said yes to, of course. And… there's a catch."

"Yeah?" Oscar wasn't good at being patient. "What is it?"

"Spencer will be there."

It took Oscar a second. "Your… Wait. That shitty ex? *What?* Why would they invite him?"

"Remember I said he was a *secret* ex?" Falcon sighed. "Came back to bite me in the ass, didn't it? Again."

"Hon, just tell them. I'm sure they'll uninvite him."

"And start asking questions about why a nineteen-year-old guy was fucking around with a sixteen-year-old."

"It's not illegal," Oscar reminded him. "And he'd be in trouble, not you. They wouldn't blame you anyway."

"Maybe they should." Silence hung between them for a few seconds before Falcon breathed out. "I didn't mean that."

"Good," Oscar breathed out. "Don't make me fly there and kick your ass. *And* his. When's the wedding?"

Falcon laughed faintly. "Yeah, I won't. Next month."

"Fuck. While I'm on my Australia/New Zealand tour. Or I'd come scare Spencer off for you. Fucker. Don't you *dare* sleep with him."

"It's okay. I'll resist the temptation," Falcon answered dryly. "I've met broken clocks with better rhythm than him."

Truth be told, the sex had been great for a closeted teen just discovering that dicks were where it was at, but since then? Even the assholes out there who ghosted him after a fuck were better in bed than Spencer had been.

And then there was the refusal to come out to anyone,

and dumping Falcon when he put his foot down and said it had to go one way or the other. It was fair enough—he was entitled to make his own choices about being miserably closeted—but Falcon couldn't let himself get dragged into that place. It might have felt good for Spencer to pretend his other football buddies didn't know he sucked dick on the weekends, but Falcon wasn't going to hide himself.

The weird hot-and-cold treatment, the refusal to talk about anything in the future, the weird chill that came over him after sex… all of that stemmed from Spencer's fears. And Falcon was way, *way* past that stage of his life.

He'd finally realized he was waiting for someone to rescue him, and he'd screwed up his courage and rescued his own damn self.

"And now he's back," he mumbled, half to himself.

Oscar clicked his tongue. "I don't like it. Walking in there with nobody knowing? No. Can you tell your sister?"

"I don't want to tell anyone about *us*. We broke up. That's in the past. Am I gonna come out to them? Yeah. I'd like to."

"At the wedding?" Oscar gasped.

"Maybe. If I bring a male date. They kept bugging me, asking which it would be. They *know*. We all know. It's, like, the worst-kept secret since the case of the vanishing cucumber, in oh-nine."

"What—no, actually," Oscar cut himself off. "Beside the point."

"It was *definitely* me that took it."

"Didn't need to know that. The point is, at your sister's wedding?"

"Oh, god, yes. She's even more… er… melodramatic than me. She'll *love* it. She keeps trying to, like, drop hints that I can bring whoever I want, even 'just a friend'."

"Even if she weren't a lesbian, I'd already be questioning why the hell you haven't just told them."

"Because then it becomes a *thing*," Falcon sighed. "And in my family, a *thing* is open for public input and help. They'll find nice boys to set me up with, and give me the gay safe sex talk, and Mom will want to do a *it's a gay* party. En-gay-gement. I bet you twenty bucks she'll do it."

Oscar was laughing. "Man, your family."

"Is a little weird," Falcon admitted. "But yeah. I've been thinking, just grab some random guy, bring him as a date, get it out of the way with, and then tell them I'm dating some-one… and avoid family functions where they'll expect him to be there… for a while… maybe forever…"

"I see the holes."

"Stop spying on my bedroom, then."

"Jesus. Falcon. You're gross," Oscar laughed.

"No, you." Falcon paused. "Miss you. Do you get to come home before Australia?"

"Yeah, we get a couple days off."

"Awesome. Tell me ASAP when they are so I can front-load work and be free." Falcon's gaze wandered across his studio to his desktop computer. He was out of the zone to work on the painting now. He might as well spend the after-noon on digital art.

"Okay. Love you, babe. Don't fuck your ex," Oscar bade.

"You too. Don't fuck your feet. Unless you're into that—" The phone line clicked and Falcon laughed, pushing himself away from the counter to wash his hands more thoroughly.

Blane. It made sense. But how the hell was he gonna bring it up without sounding totally weird? That was a problem for a bowl of instant chicken and rice and a bottle of wine tonight.

CHAPTER
Eight
BLANE

GROCERY SHOPPING COMBINED TWO OF BLANE'S LEAST favorite things: people, and waiting for them to stop being dumb. He gritted his teeth as yet another middle-aged lady glued to her iPhone cut him off, meandering in front of the aisle entrance. She stopped there to admire whatever was on her screen.

Oh my god. Get me out of here.

Blane huffed loudly and pointedly, but the lady didn't pay him any attention, just wandered slowly forward, still glued to her phone as he waited.

When he could get by, he made a beeline for the chips and stuffed them into his cart, then looked around. Anything else? Dammit, he'd forgotten cheese.

Back to the coolers, around more groups of people milling around as if they had no idea what food was or how to prepare it, and he grabbed cheddar cheese.

"Fancy meeting you here."

Before he snapped at whoever it was, Blane turned to see.

Oh. His jaw almost dropped. Falcon. In a moment, his

mood was jolted away, cleared as if a ray of sun had broken through the angry gray clouds above. "H-Hey."

"Sorry, didn't mean to scare you," Falcon laughed, his voice light. He seemed constantly cheerful—he'd hardly been without a smile, except when he was absorbed in his work.

Meanwhile, Blane was very conscious of his stiff expression. He tried on a smile in return, fingers curling tightly around the handlebar of his shopping cart. He was suddenly self-conscious of its contents.

Falcon's eyes drifted down to it for a moment, and then he nodded to his own basket. "We have the same tastes. I tried keto a few months ago, but I just about ate the muffin man."

There he went again, startling a laugh out of Blane before he knew it. "That would be a shame."

"Mmm." Falcon winked. "So I've relaxed a bit, but it's hard not to slip up. I end up in the gym working off those pretzels…"

Blane blushed, thinking of the chips front and center in his cart. "Yeah. Exactly."

"So, are you stalking me?"

It took a second for that to sink in. Blane's brows furrowed. "I… what? No."

Falcon waggled his phone at him. "I saw the distance when you messaged me the other day. Less than a mile? We must live close by."

"Oh." Blane hadn't even thought to check Falcon's Grindr profile again when messaging. "That's… sort of creepy. Are *you* stalking *me*?"

"Technically, the app is. I'm just observing the data it provides," Falcon grinned, and Blane chuckled.

"Okay, I'll let you off."

There was an awkward pause as Blane realized that he'd now become one of those assholes cutting off everyone who was trying to get to the cheese cooler.

Oh well. Motherfuckers were standing exactly in my way for the last half-hour. They can wait thirty seconds to get their precious Brie.

"Maybe I don't want you to let me off," Falcon countered with a grin. "You have a number?"

"A… phone… yes. I mean, uh, sure." Blane wasn't used to cute, eager, and forthright in one package. Just thinking that word made him flush with heat as he swapped phones with Falcon to type his number in.

"There." Falcon beamed at him. "Now I can stop worrying Grindr will fuck up."

Blane relaxed again and laughed under his breath. "Yeah. It does that sometimes, doesn't it?"

"God. You ever lose all your fucking conversations before? What a pain in the ass."

Blane winced. "Yeah. And when you accidentally block someone…"

"And you have to decide whether you unblock everyone you've ever blocked, just to get them back? I did that once." Falcon groaned. "Cue every fifty-something married daddy looking for a *pretty smooth twink slave.*"

Holy shit. Falcon had said that in public, in the middle of the grocery store? Blane was turning bright red, but he couldn't remember the last time he'd laughed so richly. He was a little too buff to attract that kind of attention, but he knew the guys Falcon meant. "Or every gold-digger who thinks that vets make a lot of money. Weird, huh?"

"What?" Falcon furrowed his brows. "They do? Dude, try being an artist. That'll solve your problem. It's basically code for unemployed. Eligible but shallow men scatter like bachelorette parties at a leather night."

An older couple nearby stared at them and walked quickly away, as if afraid they had smallpox or something.

Blane had to lean on his cart, he was laughing so hard. Falcon's grin was bright and unrepentant. And yeah, he'd briefly thought *unemployed* too, but he'd given Falcon a chance and learned better.

They walked together down the nearest aisle, not really looking at the shelves around them. "Just about done shopping?" Falcon asked.

"Yeah. That was it. You?"

"A couple more things. Peanut butter, good source of protein. Pineapple, in case I get lucky…"

Blane's cheeks were on fire, but he found himself strangely not caring who overheard. At least the bastards gave them space now. "This is a great shopping strategy."

"What, be loudly gay and watch them flee in terror? It works on the bus, too. If you need elbow room, start scrolling through Grindr," Falcon winked. "Ah, man. When I got my own car… everything got better."

"I had one since I was, like, sixteen," Blane chuckled. It was pretty middle-class of him, but his parents had bought him one.

"Lucky. I had a boyfriend with one…" Falcon trailed off, scrutinizing him for a second as if to see if he was okay with the reference. Of course he was. He had no right to be jealous over a guy he'd just gotten the number of.

"Yeah?"

Falcon grimaced. "He was a dick in the end, but at least he drove me places. Mostly his dorm, so we could fool around without my parents finding out." He was laughing again.

"Sorry," Blane frowned. "Your parents don't know?"

"Funny story, actually," Falcon laughed. They were almost at the checkouts. He looked at them, then back at Blane. "But maybe I'll save it for the date."

"Oh. The date," Blane repeated, trying not to sound dumb. His expression brightened. "Yeah. That's only a few days now. Are you coming to the zoo again before then?"

"I thought I might. Unlimited membership, baby," Falcon laughed. "And you could use some cheering up at work, huh?"

"Who said I needed cheering up?"

"Your face says it all." Falcon reached out to pinch his chin and pulled a mock-stern face. "Yelling at the poor visitors…"

Blane slapped his hand away but chuckled. "*Yelling* is a bit harsh. I might have told you off…"

"All growly while you did. Rrrawr." Falcon unloaded his cart onto the checkout aisle while Blane stood there, not even sure how to react.

Falcon poked him in the stomach with the end of the checkout divider, then slapped it on the belt.

Wordlessly, Blane unpacked the cart while Falcon chuckled at him.

He was just so… *out there*. Sure, he'd met outgoing guys before. He could be outgoing himself in the right circumstances. But Falcon seemed determined to coax laughter out of him and everyone around.

Falcon was kind of adorable.

And he had a dick ex? This didn't sound like a great story for a first date, but Blane was willing to wait if Falcon wasn't ready to talk about it yet. That did give him pause to think for a second, though.

He's hitting on me, for sure. But for more than sex? I don't know. Don't come on too strong, if he's had a bad experience. It doesn't seem that bad, though, since he's laughing about it.

Falcon made the checkout clerk laugh by talking about his reusable bags, and then stood nearby, waiting for Blane to check out. Once they were out of the store, Falcon broke his reverie by snapping his fingers.

"Yoohoo. Earth to Blane. So, *did* you find everything you're looking for?"

The question made Blane smile, but he tilted his head. "What?"

Falcon sighed at him and rolled his eyes. "What are you looking for?"

"*Oh.*" This question. Blane cleared his throat. "I, uh… I don't know. Fun, dates, see what happens. I want a relationship sometime, but with the right guy."

"And you'll never know the right guy until you test a few out, huh?" Falcon grinned at him.

"Well, yeah. How else do you know your chemistry? If you don't click in bed…" Blane trailed off. Did that come off as shallow? "That's not important to some people, but to me it is."

"Oh, yeah. Me too." Falcon slowed his cart, nodding as they approached a small silver hatchback. "There's my car. So, what are you doing after this?"

"After this?" Blane looked around into the dark evening as if it would offer up answers. "Uh. Nothing?"

Falcon opened the hatch of his trunk to load groceries in. "What would you *like* to be doing?"

"Are you…" Blane trailed off, his cheeks flushing. "Picking me up in a grocery store?"

"No. A parking lot. Much classier." Falcon winked and

rolled the cart into the cart return next to him, then slammed the hatch, making Blane jump. "Or trying, anyway. Is it working?"

Now that Falcon had suggested it, Blane couldn't get his mind off the idea. "Shit. I mean, yeah. I mean, I was waiting for, like, a date…"

"If you'd rather wait," Falcon shrugged. "If you're looking for a relationship and all that…"

Blane was a little too fast off the mark. "No." He blushed. "I mean, uh, nah. I like fooling around." *Desperate much? Come on, Blane.*

"Come over, then. I'll text you my address in like, half an hour." Before he knew it, Falcon leaned in to press a kiss against Blane's lips. His lips were soft and warm, and goddamn, he smelled good.

Then he pulled away and winked, got into his car, and Blane managed, "See you soon." He tried to shake himself out of the reverie and walk to his own car and play it cool.

So much for cool. I think I blew cool, like, fifteen minutes ago. He looked over his shoulder to watch Falcon pull out of the parking lot.

He took out his phone and turned the ringer to full volume.

CHAPTER
Nine

FALCON

Blane's knock on the door came just as Falcon shoved the last of the dry dishes into the cupboard. He paused to take one more look around his little place, making sure it looked respectable, then hurried to the door to open up.

"Hey—whoa." Blane's eyes were drawn over Falcon's shoulder, then back to his face. "Cool place."

Falcon relaxed and grinned. "You think? It's so stereotypical."

"Yeah, but it suits you," Blane told him, and Falcon stepped aside to let him inside.

There was a certain something between them now that they both knew why Blane was there, but Falcon resisted the urge to jump on Blane yet. This wasn't the usual Grindr hookup where shoes were barely off before shirts.

Blane wanted to take him on a date. Or at least, had wanted to until he'd suggested this. It remained to be seen if he'd fade off the map like every other guy. Falcon brushed the thought aside. If the sex was hot enough, surely it was worth it.

"Want a beer?" Falcon abruptly offered. That seemed like a good way to break the tension.

"Yeah, sure."

He grabbed cans from the fridge as Blane followed him into the main living space, stopping in the center of the room to turn around. Presumably he was admiring the art everywhere. At least, Falcon hoped so.

They clinked beer cans and cracked them open. "To beginnings," Blane said simply, then drank.

It took Falcon a moment to mirror him. *Beginnings of what?* But then, that question might only be answered over time.

"I really like your style," Blane said.

In the middle of his studio, where the ceiling was the highest, Falcon had his drying area. The windows and fan in this place were more than adequate to vent paint fumes in the early stages. About half the place was filled with stacks of completed works, easels, and a workspace for his work-in-progress.

"Thanks." Falcon watched Blane wander through the space, especially eyeing the beer can in his hand. Surely a vet had a good sense of balance. "The meerkat one is in progress over there."

"I just saw! Wow, it's almost done, isn't it?"

Falcon joined Blane next to the easel and nodded. "Wedding's in a couple weeks. I want to make sure it's ready for the big day. Curing takes time."

"Oh. Makes sense." Blane drank deeply and shook his head. "I'd never be able to do it."

"Everyone says that." Falcon hooked his thumb through his belt loop. "Just takes practice, like anything. I wouldn't be able to inoculate a bunch of otters without practice."

Blane laughed, his gaze wandering across the line of paintings leaning against the wall. "Yeah. Why are these not in galleries and stuff? Or your portfolio online?"

"Sales are slow…" Falcon trailed off, tilting his head. "My portfolio?" he repeated.

Blane turned red and cleared his throat, then swigged his beer again. "I, uh, might have Googled you."

"The disadvantage of having a weird name," Falcon chuckled. "That's my painting business. That's half my work life."

"What's the other half? If you don't mind saying," Blane added.

Falcon cracked a smile. "My X-rated art. No, digital art. Cutesy cartoons with feel-good sayings."

"Oh," Blane laughed. "Disappointing."

"Thanks!" Falcon snorted and elbowed him, then headed to the couch to sit down. Being around Blane had this dizzying effect, and he wasn't sure what to make of it.

Blane followed and gave him an adorable crooked grin. "Welcome." He crashed close to Falcon and put his arm along the back of the sofa, behind him. "If you *did* paint X-rated art, what would it be about?"

"I have before." Falcon laughed. "Commissions online, while I was putting myself through art school. That ain't cheap. D'you know how many dicks I had to draw? It's not very titillating anymore."

"Titillating," Blane repeated with a snicker. "Sorry. Half my mental age is waiting outside the door, apparently."

Falcon laughed again and finished his beer, then set the can aside as he watched Blane tip his head back to do the same. Stubble grazed his chin and drew his eyes to his lips, then down to his throat.

Blane set aside his can and looked at Falcon, who met his gaze and didn't look away. It was a nonverbal agreement, much like usual, to stop talking and start making out.

They leaned in at the same moment. Hands slid over each other's knees, then shoulders and the backs of necks, awkwardly getting a grip on each other's bodies.

Their lips met, warm and gentle at first, exploratory. Blane seemed to be taking it carefully, cupping Falcon's cheek and stroking his cheekbone with his thumb. It was nice to be treated gently for a change, rather than rushing to the main act.

Falcon leaned into the heat of Blane's body, slowly sliding toward him until their legs were pressed from hip to knee. His back would hurt if they kept this angle up for long, though, so he shifted to slide his knee over Blane's lap.

"You look good there."

Falcon grinned at Blane and tipped his chin up with a finger, leaning down slowly and deliberately for another kiss. "I know I do."

"You know where you'd look even better?"

He knew what any man would say now. "On your dick?"

Blane's eyes crinkled in amusement. "Yeah. But I was gonna say fucking my mouth." He pressed a mischievous kiss against Falcon's lips. "Your call."

"Oh." Falcon's breath rushed out. "I... wouldn't mind that." His voice was strained as he tried to keep it from cracking. That was the understatement of his life.

Blane had ignited passion in him that he'd forgotten. It was more than the passing physical interest and sex just for the hell of it. The chemistry was strangely unbearable. It made him itch for more, and at the same time, he felt... vulnerable.

And being offered a blowjob before anything else? It had been a while. But it fit with what little he'd guessed of Blane's nature: dependable, invested in caring for the few people (or mostly animals, if he was like many vets) he actually cared about, and sexually confident.

It was an intoxicating mix. Falcon's whole body ached for anything of Blane's touch: his cock in him, yeah, but also his hands on his back or playing with his hair, his lips grazing his chest or ear or neck, his tongue sliding between his lips.

Falcon hardly knew how to express what he wanted, so he settled for what he was offered. He slid carefully off Blane's lap, swaying and grabbing the back of the couch as Blane leaned forward to unzip and unbutton his jeans.

He was hard already, and Blane took care as he slid down his clothes to reveal just *how* turned on Falcon was.

"Gorgeous," Blane whispered, scooting to the edge of the sofa and wrapping his hand around Falcon's hip to pull him close.

"Flattery will get you everywhere," Falcon laughed, but his breath hitched.

Blane was already leaning in to run his tongue around the head in slow, tantalizing circles. The wet heat was a tease, a promise of what was to come, and Falcon dug his nails into the back of the couch to avoid begging. Yet.

Blane's broad hand wrapped around the length, stroking from base to tip before he leaned down to press kisses against Falcon's balls.

Falcon's knees weakened as Blane took one into his mouth, gently pressing his lips into sensitive skin, then the other, before kissing his way up the seam along the underside of his shaft.

"You're patient," Falcon muttered, trying and failing not to make it sound like a complaint.

Blane chuckled. "When the payoff is worth it." He swiped his tongue along the sensitive spot where head met shaft, then wrapped his lips tightly around the shaft and pushed his head down.

Feeling himself glide into Blane's mouth, in and out of the wet, tight heat, made Falcon grab the sofa harder, bending over slightly and widening his stance as much as he could with his jeans around his shins. "Oh, God."

Blane moaned appreciatively, and the vibrations coursed down Falcon's sensitive shaft, making his skin ignite. Electric charges of need curled his toes and fingers, sparked at his nipples, and even his lips felt sensitive to the gasped breaths across them.

Falcon pulsed with need already. "Ooof. Oh, fuck. Blane." The urge to move was almost irresistible.

Blane dug his nails into Falcon's hip and pulled him sharply in, almost making him fall onto his face if he hadn't had such a tight grip on the sofa. The encouragement was all Falcon needed to thrust, slowly at first, then faster until he matched the pace Blane had been setting.

The slight ridges of the roof of his mouth, the tightness of the head fitting into Blane's throat, and even Blane's strong grip on him made Falcon breathless, his world narrowing to just this pleasure.

"Yes… I'm so close," Falcon panted, straightening up again. He held onto the sofa with one hand, the back of Blane's head with the other. It was impossible to tell him how goddamn good he was without sounding repetitive, so he let his moans do the job.

And then he was tightening, drawing so near the edge he could hardly hold on. "Blane," he breathed out, pulling back.

Blane let him go, but he held onto Falcon tightly and leaned in to lap at the head while Falcon stroked. "I don't mind."

"You... don't?" Falcon's voice was a gasp even to his own ears, but he was out of energy to hold back.

"Let me." Blane leaned in again, and it only took one smooth, tight glide of his lips from head to base before Falcon was squirming, pushing, letting go of all that heat that had built up in quick, needy thrusts. And true to his word, Blane swallowed, his throat working around the head, which made Falcon whimper with pleasure.

"Oh, my god." Falcon faintly breathed a laugh and pulled back when he'd gone still, the urge to thrust melting into boneless bliss. "Fuck. Wow." Blane pulled him down to sit on the couch and he gladly went. "Thanks...?"

Blane laughed. "You're welcome. I'm glad I was that good."

"A lot of guys..." Falcon said, his tongue loosened by the stupefying pleasure throbbing in his body, then trailed off.

"Hm?"

"Just wanna fuck me. Don't even wanna get me off, you know?" Falcon rolled his eyes. "Mostly those asshole alpha dudes. It's all about them."

"I don't see who wouldn't want to worship that gorgeous body." Blane ran his hand up Falcon's stomach and chest, pulling his shirt up as he went, and moaned appreciatively at the shape he was in. "You're sexy when you come."

"O-Oh." Falcon was blushing and he knew it. His head spun as he tried to clamp down on his tongue before he said anything even more stupid and clingy. "I… Thanks. Your turn."

Blane laughed, his hand wrapping around Falcon's and lacing fingers. "You look half-asleep."

"Not too asleep for that." Falcon walked his fingers, awkward though it was, along Blane's thigh before Blane stopped him, flattening his hand against his thigh. "Mm?"

"That one was for you."

Blane's boner was clear as daylight through his jeans, and now that Falcon was looking at it, he couldn't take his eyes off it. "Please?"

"What?"

Falcon said it as plainly as he could: "I love sucking cock. I wanna suck yours. Unless you want me to wait." Blane's grip on his hand weakened, and he knew he was in. "It'd be a shame to let that load go to waste."

"You have a way with words," Blane told him and pulled his hand back, lacing his hands behind his head for a moment and stretching.

Falcon rolled sideways to stretch along the couch on his front, his face in Blane's crotch already. "Thank God you said yes. I didn't want to have to beg."

"I don't often meet a guy who likes sucking dick as much as me," Blane laughed deeply.

"It's better than anal in some ways."

"Yeah," Blane nodded, lighting up.

"A hell of a lot easier. More versatile. Quicker when you're on the go…" Falcon unzipped Blane's jeans and slid his fingers in through the fly, rubbing the shaft a few times before he unbuttoned them and worked that manhood free.

"Are you suggesting public fucking?" Blane exclaimed.

"I'm not *not* suggesting it," Falcon grinned coyly up at Blane, and he earned a tweak to his ear.

"Sweet, bubbly, and surprisingly kinky. Noted."

Falcon snickered, pushing Blane's underwear out of the way. "Oooh. Look at *that*." Blane was hard already and his girth filled Falcon's grip. If he hadn't just come, he'd be horny just at the sight of it.

"Way with words," Blane muttered again, looking pleased. He spread his arms along the back of the couch, gripping on either side of himself.

Falcon licked slowly from those heavy balls up the shaft, tasting the musk of him with pleasure. He loved giving head exactly as much as he'd told Blane. Whatever the guys who were too manly to suck dick thought about it, the control was completely in his hands, and he could make Blane come undone with his hands and mouth alone. Blane was already halfway there. He really had loved it, too.

That was the sexiest feeling in the world.

His shaft was pink and throbbing under Falcon's teases, but Falcon didn't let that stop him from teasing a bit more. He pinched the loose skin gently between his lips, then swiveled his head back and forth around the head, sucking gently at first, then harder.

"*Oh*," Blane grunted. "Nnn—Nice."

Falcon shifted himself to get a better angle, then pushed his head down on the shaft, taking his time to let the girth of him slide across his tongue all the way to the back of his throat. When he was sure he wasn't going to choke, he pulled his head up and pushed down again.

Blane's hips kept jerking up in desperate little pushes before he settled again, so he didn't waste more time teasing.

He sucked fast and hard, intending to blow Blane's mind at that pace.

Blane was doing a good job keeping his hands off. *Ever the gentleman, then.* Falcon ran his hand up Blane's stomach and under his shirt to tweak a nipple, rubbing gently with a thumb and listening for the catches and growls in Blane's breathing.

Then he got it loose of his shirt and ran his hand over his shoulder and biceps to pull against his hand, guiding it to his head.

"You don't mind?" Blane whispered. "I know I'm…"

Big? Oh, yeah, he is. How sweet. Falcon tried not to chuckle. His mouth was a little too full for coherent noises. He nodded slightly and tightened his grip on Blane's hand before releasing it to wrap his hand around the base of the shaft.

Blane fucked his mouth in staccato thrusts, his head rolling back against the back of the sofa. "Oh, fuck. Yes!"

Feeling Blane lose himself in pleasure was so goddamn sexy that even Falcon felt heat prickle his skin. When Blane tried to pull him away, he resisted and swallowed. He didn't usually swallow on a first date, but to reciprocate? Hell yeah.

He sucked Blane clean, pulling his mouth slowly off his softening dick and casting a last sultry glance up at Blane from his lap.

Blane was watching him with a strange look on his face: something affectionate, maybe? No, that was just the orgasm talking. His *and* Blane's.

"Wow," Blane whispered. "You're pretty great yourself. I'm glad I came over."

"Less *over* and more *in*," Falcon smirked, pushing himself upright and licking his lips.

Blane laughed, then pulled him in for a loose, easy kiss. No pressure, no expectation. Just… yeah, that was kind of affectionate.

Falcon let himself lean into Blane's chest for a good minute before asking the question. "So, this weekend…?"

"Hm?" Blane seemed confused for a moment, and Falcon's heart started sinking. "Oh! The wine and auction. What, can you still make it?"

"Did you want me to?"

"Why wouldn't I?" Blane straightened up, his arm tightening around Falcon's shoulders.

Falcon laughed. *No way am I getting neurotic on him after the best orgasm ever.* "I can make it. Just making sure."

"Arranging your schedule of suitors?" Blane grinned at him.

Falcon hesitated, then admitted, "There aren't many."

"Mm. Right." Blane nodded slightly, eyeing him. He couldn't tell what Blane was thinking as he pushed himself up to his feet slowly and tucked himself away. "I better get going, though."

Stay. But Falcon didn't say it out loud. He just smiled casually, trying with all his might not to let the hopes that had risen take over his thinking. "Yeah? It's almost the weekend anyway."

"Mmm. I better save up my stamina."

"For hot sex afterward?"

"That and interacting with actual people beforehand." Blane wrinkled his nose.

"I'm people."

"You're sexy people." Blane wagged a finger. "There's a difference."

Falcon laughed, charmed despite himself. *Fuck it. I like him. It's too late not to.* "Okay. I'm flattered."

He saw Blane to the door in a whirlwind of thoughts, and just like in the parking lot, before he left, Blane leaned in for a little kiss.

Falcon caught himself pressing his hand to his mouth after the door was closed, leaning against it and shutting his eyes. All signs pointed to him being stupid again, assuming a guy he'd specifically enticed here on the promise of no-strings-attached sex might want... well, more afterward. Which he *knew* was the dumbest hope to have when dating.

The tighter he held on, the quicker anything—or anyone—slipped out of his grasp.

But Blane acted kind of like he did want more, all... considerate, even a touch romantic. And if he kept *that* up, Falcon could maybe find a balance between what he wanted and what the surly hunk was willing to give. Maybe he didn't need a happily-ever-after, if Blane could be happy like this for a while.

I could get used to this. Really dangerously used to this.

CHAPTER
Ten

BLANE

"HE DOESN'T HAVE SUITORS. HE DOESN'T WANT THEM. GO easy."

Blane cursed at himself as his hand slipped on the tie knot again. He was so fucking out of practice with these things. Maybe he'd look better without one anyway. If Falcon wasn't wearing one, he might feel awkward otherwise.

Blane tossed it aside and unbuttoned the top button of his shirt, then turned in the mirror. Simple navy blue button-down shirt and trousers, both ironed specifically for the occasion.

If he didn't leave now, he was going to be late to pick up Falcon. That thought drove him toward the door, double-checking that he had everything.

He normally worried about his appearance before a date, but he'd taken even more time than usual tonight. He didn't dare to think about why.

Falcon was already waiting by the time he pulled up to

the curb and he frowned apologetically as his date climbed in. "Sorry, were you waiting long?"

"Not at all." Falcon beamed at him and leaned across the seat. Halfway to a kiss, he froze, as if realizing he wasn't sure what the etiquette was.

Blane had frozen for a second, too, out of sheer surprise. But it made sense, with the way Falcon threw himself into everything with cheer and determination: painting, blowjobs, maybe life. That kind of energy was nice to be around. He leaned in and closed the gap to peck Falcon's lips. "Good evening to you, too."

Falcon grinned sheepishly and buckled up. "Hope you don't mind."

"I can categorically state I wouldn't mind your lips literally anywhere."

"Anywhere?"

Gears in Falcon's brain were turning, and Blane was equally aroused and worried. Why did he have the feeling that, if he were with Falcon, this would be a constant state of mind? Blane narrowed his eyes. "Probably anywhere. Don't put that to the test."

"Aww," Falcon sighed and folded his arms. "I'll keep my lips to myself in public. How was your day?"

"Quiet. Weekends usually are, when I'm not seeing my friends. I get errands done and walk around town, that's about it." *And clean my house in case I get laid tonight.* "You?"

Falcon groaned. "Work and more work. I don't want to talk about it."

Blane nodded sympathetically. He occasionally had to pull overtime hours when animals were gravely ill, in labor, or just settling in. But overall, the zoo hours were short enough that it was a simple full-time job. He couldn't imagine the pressure Falcon lived under, and his respect for the man's cheeriness despite his circumstances edged up. "That's… a hard job."

"It's what I love. But you're right, it can be." Before he could answer, Falcon went on. "But it's a hundred times better than some boring 9-to-5 job. No offense."

"I was just thinking how horrible it must be to always be working," Blane admitted with a laugh. "But then, I'm one to talk. My hours do get weird sometimes. This one time a couple weeks ago…" *Wait. Do you talk to a guy about a hookup on a first date?* His cheeks flushed.

"I smell gossip. Maybe embarrassing gossip. Spill," Falcon ordered, then nudged him in the ribs with his elbow. "Before I make you."

"That sounds… oddly enticing." Blane winked. "Fine. I was coming back from a first date, it seemed to go all right, but he was really pushing for sex. Which… well, you know me."

"Easily enticed?" Falcon teased.

Blane grinned. "When the words are right. We got to my house, and… ah, the other detail… I was looking after Sheila. Our baby sloth. She was asleep in the kitchen and he was a little freaked out by that."

Falcon gasped. "That must have been adorable! I saw her last week. Isn't she only on loan temporarily or something?"

Blane reeled for a moment—instead of laughing, Falcon had gone into *adorable animal* mode. His hands were clasped together tightly, his voice higher. "What? I mean. Uh. Yeah. But it was kind of funny."

"Oh yeah," Falcon laughed. "But I wouldn't be weirded out at all. As long as she was fast asleep…"

"I think I like you." Blane kept his voice as light as possible, but the comment probably still came off more… well… *revealing* than he'd wanted it to.

"Good. You should." Falcon grinned cheekily at him. "So there's definitely a wine corner here, right?"

"There's a wine corner. And h'ors d'oeuvres."

"I vote we hang out there."

"That's exactly what I do, when I bother going," Blane admitted. "It's more fun with someone else."

Falcon hummed. "Even though I'm, you know… I've always said I'm happily single… I get that. Especially living alone. You do too, huh? Aside from sloth visitors?"

"Yeah," Blane chuckled. "The peace and quiet is nice, but sometimes prolonged."

They moved on to talk about the weather and what was on the radio as Blane took them to the parking lot of the zoo. Luckily, both of them lived close by to it for different reasons—Blane because it was his workplace, Falcon because he'd got a studio apartment years ago while the rent was cheap and the landlord liked him enough to keep him around, he said.

That led them to talking about housing and renting versus mortgages as Blane handed over his tickets and offered Falcon his arm.

Falcon broke off in the middle of an opinionated sentence about houses being a liability and stared at him, then around. "You're…?"

Right. Shit. He wasn't out. Blane winced at the mistake. "Sorry, I'm not used to—" But before he could lower his arm, Falcon took it.

"Don't take liberties," Falcon warned him, his eyes sparkling. "I might just allow it."

Blane didn't know what to say, so he just led Falcon for the wine.

"We're at the heavy drinking stage of the first date already, huh?" Falcon accepted the wine glass and clinked it against Blane's, and they found a corner out of the way of the people who actually seemed interested in buying art. "This asshole ex I once had. Oh. Uh."

"What?"

"I don't think you're supposed to tell asshole ex stories on a first date," Falcon grinned, looking sideways at him.

"I don't think you're supposed to tell Grindr first date stories on a first date, either." Blane smirked. "And technically, you *could* count it as our second. You may as well spill the beans now."

"If that counts as a date..." Falcon snickered.

Blane hummed. "Well, I'd count it. I saw your place, you showed me your art. And then..."

"Huh. I suppose." Falcon laced his fingers with Blane's for a moment, then let go. "I'm just not used to there being another date afterward. Like we said."

"Like we said," Blane agreed in a murmur. "So, that ex?"

"Oh, right." Falcon rolled his eyes. "He just brought me to an event at his school once, some scholarship banquet. But he was closeted—and I mean *really* closeted—so he barely looked at me. People thought I was his little brother."

Blane laughed. "Awkward. How long did you date him?"

"About two years. I turned eighteen and... well, the closet thing got too much." Falcon glanced earnestly at him. "So yeah, I'm fine being on your arm. Everyone *knows* anyway. They're just waiting for me to actually say it."

"That must be nice, though. Knowing they're waiting and being supportive, huh?"

"And your family...?" Then Falcon winced. "Yeah, that's probably not first date conversation either."

"I think we already blew past that." Falcon stared at him, his cheeks reddening, and didn't seem to know what to say. He shook his head, then almost spilled his wine as he finished it.

Blane laughed and let him refill. When he came back, Blane told him, "But yeah, mine took adjustment. I wasn't sure, before I did. I was just about to leave for vet school then. Nervous as all hell. But it worked out in the end. We don't talk much, but just because... I'm an adult and I've got my own life, you know how it is. We're not close, as a family. But they're good now."

Falcon slipped his hand into Blane's again, and this time, he held it. "Good."

"I'm glad you don't mind weird first-date stories. Like being mistaken for brothers. That's really weird, isn't it?" Falcon laughed.

"Only if you fucked afterward. Did you?" Falcon's sideways glance told him the answer. "Oh my god, you did."

"I was staying in his dorm room! We were teens! Privacy, you know? We weren't *not* gonna take advantage..."

Blane laughed. "So what do you want people here to think of us as?"

He hadn't expected the question to make Falcon get so flustered, but he did. His grip tightened on Blane's hand for a moment and he cleared his throat, looking around for h'ors d'oeuvres or some form of rescue.

Blane's chest tightened. *Is that a good thing or a bad one? I can't tell.* Either way, he knew how he was going to end the evening now.

Before Falcon could come up with an answer, the

auctioneer tapped the microphone and tested it, and then the auction was in full swing.

Falcon never answered the question, but he hardly let go of Blane's hand all evening, either.

CHAPTER
Eleven

FALCON

IT HAD BEEN A LONG FUCKING TIME SINCE ANYONE DROPPED Falcon off at home with just a goodnight kiss and didn't ghost him immediately.

He'd watched his phone breathlessly for the next couple hours, picking it up just to check he could still see Blane's profile and his online texting status. It seemed like Blane *was* the kind of guy he'd taken him for—slow-moving unless pressed, and sincere. Falcon gradually relaxed as he realized that if Blane weren't interested, he would have told him that straight-up.

Which meant he didn't want to rush into sex, and that was... kind of sweet. The novelty factor alone kept Falcon interested. That was half the thrill—the anticipation—and he was willing to let Blane get away with it until the second date. Or third. However the hell they were counting these things.

If a blowjob is a first date, and a wine-and-dine evening with just a kiss is the second, do I jump his bones on the third? I don't know the rule for this.

Falcon was so distracted that he nearly bent the bristles of one of his favorite brushes as he cleaned it in spirits. He cursed under his breath as he realized what his hands were doing. That was the other thing: Blane was on his mind now…

All. The. Time.

It was kind of exhausting, and kind of exhilarating, and he wanted it to continue.

The moment his phone rang, Falcon's heart soared, and he realized he was hoping it was Blane.

Goddamn. I've got it bad.

It wasn't. He didn't recognize the number, so he shrugged, thumbed it, and answered. Couldn't afford to miss a business opportunity. "Hello?"

He'd recognize the snake-oil tones that slid from his phone speaker anywhere. Spencer. It had to be.

"Falcon. Man, I had to ask around for your number. Good to hear you again."

He couldn't just hang up in the guy's face. Falcon's fuck-you attitude was wrapped in stifling politeness. "Spencer, is it?" he asked casually, like he wasn't really sure. That ought to make Spencer twitchy. He'd always been easily made jealous.

"Yeah. So I know this is out of the blue, but we're gonna be at the wedding together." Spencer's tone was just as smooth as always. He'd had a great phone sex voice, but his voice was the kind bosses and parents liked, too. God, he was good at sucking up to parents. It was how his own parents had invited him almost into the family and trusted him to take care of him when they "hung out" together.

He sure had. Not that Falcon regretted the fucking, but he could have done without the mindfucking.

"So I heard."

Spencer blew a sigh between his lips. "So we should, you know. Meet up and talk. I've got some things to say, I guess."

Is he actually trying to apologize?

"We should talk, yeah. We didn't leave off on a great note," Falcon said pointedly. Under his words was the stark reminder that he'd told Spencer to fuck off until he was willing to admit he'd been using him.

"Right, yeah. It'll be awkward, I guess."

"Not if Rosalina has anything to do with it," Falcon said, staying determinedly cheery.

"I got the unofficial invite. It said I should get the official one in the mail next week. No mention of whether there's a plus-one. I hope so. I meant it'd be awkward for us on our own, huh? So we should figure this out."

He's not doing this, is he? Falcon didn't rise to the bait, even with the subtle *our* thrown in there. "I have no idea," Falcon told him. "You'd have to ask my sister."

"Right, right. Well, are you free to have that talk? Drinks?"

Alcohol and Spencer were a bad combination. He got even more obnoxiously straight-acting around his buddies, and then mopey when he was alone. Falcon was not holding him while he sighed about how hard his life was even one more time. "When?"

"Next couple days? I mean, wedding's pretty soon. Two weeks? Three? That's real soon. Lucky I wasn't out of town." Spencer sounded as self-centered as ever, too.

Yeah, because we were all on the edge of our seats hoping you could come. Falcon rolled his eyes, but he didn't really think about it before he agreed. May as well get the first unpleasant encounter out of the way with. "Yeah, whatever. Sure. Thursday."

"Thursday night, yeah? Supper?"

"I dunno, I think I'm busy," Falcon lied. "We can grab coffee, though. Two?"

"Okay. Sounds great. See you soon." Just like the old days, there was a hint of suggestion in his tone, but it made Falcon shudder now.

"Yeah. Later." He hung up and tossed his phone on the counter, then rolled his eyes so hard he almost strained them. "Asshole."

Counting the ways in which Spencer was an asshole would take all day, so he wasn't even going to bother, but he just *was*.

But more importantly, it was Tuesday and he hadn't seen Blane since Saturday. He was supposed to head to the zoo toward the end of Blane's shift. He cared a lot more about that, because two full days without Blane had seemed strangely long.

When he thought about it that way, it was kind of a good sign. Seeing Blane was a lot more important to him than meeting up with that asshole. Blane himself was more important to him than Spencer ever had been, after just a couple weeks of talking to him, a couple of dates, a lot of text messages, and a blowjob each.

I'm not going to get sucked back into Spencer's orbit... his entourage.

It had never been about a genuine interest in *him* with Spencer. Spencer had only tried him out for convenient sex, companionship, and an ear to listen when he complained about closet problems. Not to mention the fact that he'd been willing to put up with Spencer's closeted status, because being out hadn't been important to Falcon back then.

But Blane seemed interested in his career, his opinions, and a lot more than his ass.

It's weird to be treated nicely, actually. Having not really let himself date since Spencer, Falcon realized this just hadn't come up before, but it was bound to.

It wasn't that Spencer had ever hit him, or that he'd ever said no and been ignored. It wasn't even that Spencer had emotionally blackmailed him, or talked about him behind his back. None of that had happened, or maybe he would have broken things off before turning eighteen and realizing he didn't want to keep secrets.

Hell, even the closeted thing wasn't a deal breaker. Not everyone was ready to face that kind of potential shit every single time they had to out themselves. Even Falcon hadn't technically done it, because coming out over and over to everyone was exhausting. Much easier to have a boyfriend on his arm and let that do the talking.

What had driven him away from Spencer was the utter silence, the coldness that existed between them whenever they weren't fucking. But Blane? Blane had been interested in him both sexually and platonically. He'd proven that by not insisting on sex after the date.

And to be honest, Falcon had been shocked about that. *Why* had it shocked him that a guy might want to drop him off at home and not come in? Had Spencer ever done that? Now that he thought about it... maybe not.

Falcon kept an eye on the time as he chewed his thoughts over, slowly getting himself presentable for a casual evening date with Blane.

That idea—of asking Blane to accompany him to the wedding as his plus-one—kept creeping into his head. God, even as a friend, he'd appreciate the company.

Falcon didn't yet know if Blane wanted a relationship, but it was the perfect time to show Spencer that he didn't need him. Whether he showed Spencer that he was happily single —no matter the truth about the "happily" part—or happily dating, it *was* a grudge he hadn't realized he was holding.

And it had already bled into his relationship with Blane, just by comparing them, even if Blane came out on top. Wasn't bringing Blane to the wedding using him? Especially if he didn't tell him the full story beforehand? And he wasn't sure he was ready to do that.

"Shit," he muttered under his breath as he grabbed his car keys. Instead of being annoyed that Spencer had called after all these years, he was grateful now to have seen what was going on before he could sabotage a good thing.

I hope Blane's dated more than me. I could use a hand here. But he couldn't go to Blane to tell him that he was worried he just wanted to use him to prove himself to some other asshole he didn't even care about anymore. Or to prove himself to himself. He had no idea. No, he wasn't going to ask Blane his thoughts yet.

The answer was obvious: Oscar.

Before he walked out the door, he shot him a quick text to ask if they could talk soon, then another to reassure him it was nothing bad, just a dating question. *That* ought to get a quick response out of him.

Then he took a deep breath and set it all aside to let the optimism shine once more. He tried to never leave the house in a bad attitude, or he'd just spend the rest of the day with it.

Things would work out somehow. They had to.

CHAPTER
Twelve

BLANE

EVEN THOUGH HE WAS EXPECTING FALCON, THE INSTINCTIVE *who the hell's leaning on my car?* defensiveness rose before Blane could quell it. Then he relaxed and smiled, raising a hand in a wave.

Of course it was Falcon. He hadn't stood him up yet, and he'd had the opportunity.

He'd brought clothes to change into from his work uniform, but he still felt self-conscious in his jeans and polo shirt compared to their last date. But Falcon was in jeans, too, and a clingy white t-shirt that was absolutely designed to show his body off.

"Hey, good-looking," he greeted Falcon with a grin.

Falcon grinned back at him. "Hello yourself, handsome." He patted the hood of Blane's car. "I figured I'd take a turn to drive us today. You've got a parking sticker or whatever for the lot, right?"

"Yeah. Makes sense," Blane agreed, opening the back door of his car to toss his backpack in. He locked it again, then put his keys away. "Lead on."

Falcon looped his arm through Blane's and strolled to one of the few remaining cars in the lot. "How was your work day?"

"Pretty good, thanks," Blane answered. It was unfamiliar, having someone ask him that. He was used to getting home to a quiet house and a quiet life. "Uh... what's new... not much. Routine exams, no emergencies. Sheila, the sloth, is about ready to leave for her new home."

"Aw," Falcon frowned.

"I know. But it was a temporary loan. Zoos trade animals back and forth according to veterinary needs, planned exhibits, available space..."

"Like, how does that work? You call up Nashville and go *pssst, hey, I have a hippo but I need a giraffe?*" Falcon laughed.

"Actually, pretty close," Blane grinned. "I'm not in charge of that stuff, but the people who are have a network. Kind of a bulletin board. You're not allowed to charge money, so you end up coming to a mutual agreement that, say, a small herd of zebras is worth an elephant."

"Wow." Falcon pulled away from Blane as they approached his car, a beat-up little thing. "I had no idea."

Blane grinned and ducked into the car, fitting himself carefully into the front seat. He felt too big for it, but that was a common problem with hatchbacks. It had taken days at car dealerships to pick out one of his own that he felt comfortable stretching out in. "And your day?"

"My day was... boring, I guess. Mostly digital today. I wanted to come back and sketch Sheila one more time soon, if I can ever find her awake," Falcon laughed. "People online like sloths."

"They do. We saw a lot of visitors. That factors into the value of animals... more people will come to see an elephant than a sloth, but more people will see a sloth than a zebra…"

"This is crazy. This is like a whole economy." Falcon kept his eyes on the road rather than looking over at Blane while he drove. "How cool. Thank you for telling me that."

Blane laughed. "That made your day, didn't it?"

"It did!" Falcon beamed. "This pizza place is close, isn't it?"

"Just around that corner. Yeah, and then go that way." Blane glanced around the interior of the car. Not a mess, but also not tidy. He spotted scraps of paper, business cards, a few water bottles. It was homey, not that strange kind of sterile shape that some people liked to keep their cars in. Like they were new off the lot, but without the new-car smell.

"Got a call from that asshole ex. I'm meeting up with him to, I guess, let him apologize or something," Falcon laughed. "Out of the blue, after all these years."

Blane looked over sharply in surprise, then frowned. "Huh. Nice?"

"I hope so. I don't really give a fuck anymore," Falcon laughed. "But if it makes him feel better, hey, he can go to town."

He's not stuck in the past, then. Blane nodded, trying to pretend he hadn't been assessing Falcon as a partner. "Good. I'm glad."

"The wedding is about the only other thing that's up right now," Falcon said. "Which was why he called. He's gonna be there, so he wanted to talk beforehand."

"Ahh. Yeah. This is the guy who wanted you to be a secret, right?" Blane didn't mean it to sound so critical, but Falcon seemed to appreciate it, judging by his laugh.

"Yep."

Blane shook his head. "Family stuff. So awkward."

"Right? Do yours live near?"

"No. Illinois and Kentucky," Blane answered. "After the divorce, Mom moved back closer to her parents."

"Oh. Sorry." Falcon looked over for half a second, then made the final turn into the pizza place's parking lot.

Blane smiled to himself. "It's fine. I was an adult, I got over it pretty quickly. They're happier now. Mom's got a boyfriend and Dad's picked up new hobbies, that kind of stuff."

"Better no relationship than a bad one," Falcon said. "My mom's been single since Dad walked out, ages ago. She's always said it was the best thing to happen to her."

Blane looked up quickly. "Yes. *Yes,* oh, man. So many people don't get that."

"I know," Falcon groaned. "And jump into relationships because they're afraid of being single? This is why I don't have friends. I'm too… uh… blunt."

Blane laughed. "Don't tell me, you tell them the truth instead of what they want to hear."

"Got it in one." Falcon looked rueful but grinned at Blane. "So, how does this work?"

"You wanna do the drive-in, or sit inside?"

Falcon exclaimed, "Drive-in! How many drive-in restaurants are around these days?"

"Okay," Blane laughed. "So you pick one of those spots," he guided Falcon to the spots along the edge of the lot. "And…"

"Oh man, there's an order board. Genius," Falcon nodded. Each spot had its own menu board with a call button, and the car hops brought food out on trays. "Got it."

Blane leaned in to look at the menu, though he didn't really need to. He already knew what he liked.

"Wanna split a pizza?" Falcon asked, grinning. "Is this where we find out how incompatible our toppings are?"

"I think we can find a topping combination that works for us," Blane answered, his grin widening.

Falcon nodded seriously. "I like some good toppings. But I can be flexible."

"How convenient. I like to give a good topping." Blane pointed to the board. "And on your pizza?"

"Literally whatever pizza you like," Falcon laughed. "You overestimate how picky I am."

"And we need onion rings. Unless you mind onion breath."

Falcon looked back at the menu. "They're that good?"

"They really are that good." Blane dug cash out of his wallet.

"No, I've got it—"

"It's cash only."

Falcon frowned at his wallet, then Blane. "Oh, I see. Sneaky. If you keep this up, I'll owe you... well." He winked.

"That's my plan," Blane teased.

"Mmm. Yet you didn't come in after Saturday night," Falcon teased, and Blane wasn't sure why that made him blush. "Did you?"

"Place the order," Blane grumbled. "Large number seven. Easy?"

"I like mushrooms. Sold." Falcon rolled down his window and pressed the call button, beaming at Blane as he waited for an answer. Those dimples were back, obnoxiously cute as ever. Falcon looked like he was having fun all the time, but even more so now.

It was sweet. It made Blane want to show him everything cool in the world to see that smile.

Once they'd ordered, Falcon rolled up the window again. "So, what were we saying?"

"When?"

"Just now. About what we're doing tonight after this. Whether I'm dropping you off in the parking lot, or…"

Blane's gaze flickered to Falcon's lips. He was suddenly aware of how much the confined space amplified the chemistry between them. They could neither get much further away or much closer. The seats trapped them at a distance a little too close to keep conversation clean, but too far to do anything about it.

"Or?" Blane prompted.

Falcon grinned slowly. "I was hoping you'd say that."

Blane's chest jolted with a mix of trepidation and excitement. Sure, he wanted to sleep with Falcon, but… not if that was going to be it. He didn't want the first time to be the last.

Moving pretty fucking fast, aren't you, he told himself, but he ignored that. His gut instinct was telling him it was the right move. When he actually listened to it, it worked. When he didn't, he wound up on "first dates" with guys who wanted a pretext for sex.

Falcon was more than that. Falcon *liked* him, and vice versa. Hell, they might end up as friends-with-benefits, or dating (loosely defined), or dating (officially)… there was only one way to find out.

He licked his lips. "Yeah. I was hoping, too."

Falcon pulled the lever to lean his seat back and stretched out, lacing his hands behind his head. His shirt lifted, exposing smooth belly and drawing Blane's eye for a maddening moment. "And now I guess we wait for our order."

Never had Blane been more glad he'd chosen a restaurant with quick service.

Directing Falcon to his home was easy. As it turned out, they lived within half a mile of each other, though Falcon hadn't been into his particular part of the suburban maze before.

"Oh, this is it? Cute place," Falcon complimented him as they pulled into his driveway.

Oh, the neighbors are gonna talk. Good. Let 'em.

Blane got out and led Falcon up the front walkway to his front door. He was very conscious of Falcon standing a little too close to him, his warm breath on his neck.

It made him fumble with his keys before he managed to let them inside, holding the door.

Falcon grinned, looking around. "Are we alone?"

"Strictly no sloth company or otherwise," Blane promised, making Falcon laughed. "Can I take your jacket?"

"Ever the gentleman," Falcon laughed and handed it over, then took his shoes off.

Blane showed him around the ground floor—mostly open-plan, so the tour took five seconds—and to the kitchen for water. He had the feeling they'd need the rehydration shortly.

"It's a cute little place inside, too," Falcon told him. "Nice inside and out. Like you." He was giving Blane that flirty little grin again that he hardly knew what to do with.

"How do you know? You haven't seen that much yet." Blane grinned back.

"Is that an offer?"

Blane laughed. "Well… like I said, vers top."

"Is *that* what you were saying at the pizza place?" Falcon feigned innocent. "I had no idea." He wandered closer, pinning Blane against the counter with his body and setting his glass down behind him. He rested a hand on the counter on either side of Blane.

"You minx." Blane laughed at Falcon. "I don't know what to do with you."

Falcon bounced on his toes, then leaned in to breathe into Blane's ears, "Ooh. I have some ideas. Pick me."

Blane twisted to shove his glass out of the way, then closed his hands around Falcon's narrow hips, running them slowly up his sides to his shoulders. "Oh, you do? And what are those?"

"I think you should bring me somewhere more comfortable to… discuss them in depth. In lots of depth, preferably," Falcon smirked. "Without anything in the way."

Blane growled and hoisted Falcon up against him, laughing as Falcon wrapped his arms and legs tightly around him. "I'm not carrying you up the stairs."

"Aw," Falcon sighed, pressing his lips into Blane's neck. As Blane set him on the bottom step, he turned and grinned. "You want to molest me on the stairs, don't you?"

"Guilty." Blane grabbed Falcon's ass before he could jog up the stairs out of the way.

Falcon squeaked and laughed, taking the stairs two at a time as Blane chased him. Blane couldn't even remember the last time he'd chased someone—on the playground as a kid? He'd been serious even as a kid, but something about Falcon enticed Blane to have *fun*.

Falcon was at a disadvantage, hesitating as he eyed the doors at the top of the stairs.

Blane caught up and swept him off his feet again, then maneuvered him through the doorway of his bedroom to dump him on the bed. "Gotcha."

"Just where you want me?" Falcon was breathless and flushed, his hair sticking up and t-shirt rising to expose his stomach as he stretched again, playfully wriggling under Blane.

"Bingo." Blane crawled over Falcon and hooked a finger in his t-shirt, slowly drawing it up and over his head. "This can get out of the way of my view." He had no idea where this was going tonight, and he didn't care. Any kind of sex was fine with him. He'd do anything Falcon wanted to make him feel good.

Falcon grinned. "I feel the same about your clothes. Let's get all that off, huh?"

"Agreed." Blane pulled off clothing as fast as Falcon, both of them trying to help each other but doing a more efficient job on themselves. They laughed as they tangled, kicking jeans off awkwardly. Falcon had a harder time, his jeans being skinnier, but they managed it.

Falcon was gorgeous naked, and Blane took a moment for mutual admiration, bracing himself on his hands above Falcon and pulling back to get a good look.

"Come here," Falcon murmured, yanking on his ass to make him collapse on top of him.

God, that felt good. Naked, pressed skin-to-skin, without a trace of the usual self-consciousness and nervousness of being naked with someone for the first time. Maybe because they'd already had sex last week, even swallowed... that memory had kept Blane good company in his showers ever since.

Their skin was warm, and more than anything, it felt *comfortable* here against Falcon, his hips angled so their cocks were side-by-side, his forearms braced on the bed, chests rising and falling against one another's.

And Falcon's lips were right there. His eyes settled on them for a moment before he looked Falcon in the eye again and smiled.

Falcon's eyes were half-closed, and he licked his lips. "You're so fucking hot. Kiss me."

Blane shivered with pleasure at the words and did that, letting warm skin slide along skin as their lips teased each other's. The teasing lasted seconds before it got serious, breathing heavy, tongues sliding against one another's and almost vying for dominance.

Falcon kissed hard, threw himself into it without reserve, and it was almost overwhelming for Blane. He'd always taken it slower, gently easing into it, but Falcon dragged him in all at once, gasping and desperate.

It was second nature to grind against Falcon slowly, letting their hardening lengths rub.

Falcon's moan was immediate and sharp. "Yes," he panted, his hand rising from Blane's back to the back of his head as he pulled him in for an even harder kiss.

Blane groaned as Falcon caught his lower lip and nipped it, then sucked hard. He was tempting him, driving him crazy, and Blane loved every fucking second of it.

"Fuck," he hissed once his mouth was his own again. He pressed another open-mouthed kiss of need against Falcon's lips, then slid his lips along Falcon's jaw to his ear, kissed along the earlobe, flicked his tongue sharply against it.

"Nnnh. Found it," Falcon mumbled.

"Hm?"

"The first key." Falcon smirked, but the expression was wiped off his face when Blane brought his finger up to gently run along the rim of his ear. "Fuck!"

Blane grinned, glad for this discovery.

Falcon was so sensitive... or maybe he'd been just as turned on in the anticipation that had dragged out every spark throughout their pizza date. Now, all the sparks were back at once, an explosion of frustrated need and desire they reflected back at each other.

"Nipples work too. Actually... pretty much everything works at this stage," Falcon laughed breathlessly.

Blane was careful of Falcon's erection and his own as he shifted down, kissing slowly down to his collarbone. He teased the thin skin there with more kisses, then worked his way to a nipple.

Just as promised, Falcon squirmed as soon as he closed his lips around one nub of flesh. *Oh, man, he's gonna be fun.* Blane grinned wickedly at him, then flicked his tongue there as he had Falcon's ear.

Falcon was squirming under him already, gasping for breath. "Fuck... fuck! Yes," he panted. Blane could feel him throbbing with need.

Blane repeated the particular circling of his tongue that had gotten the most results, then nipped gently while Falcon whimpered. He let his fingers continue the work on that nipple and moved to the other.

"Fucking..." Falcon groaned, his words tumbling after each other. "Can't even think..."

"I love making you swear," Blane whispered, letting cool air and his warm breath breeze over the wet skin. "You look like you're gonna burst."

"Don't you dare make me come before you..." Falcon trailed off.

"Before I do what to you?" Blane prompted, curious what Falcon wanted.

"I don't even know what I want. Fuck. More of that, *please*, but more, too..." Falcon covered his mouth when Blane brushed his lips faintly across the nipple. "Oh, God!"

Blane sucked harder, pinching and rolling the other nipple until Falcon's body arched clear off the bed.

With this kind of response, how could he *not* want to move his lips elsewhere? Despite his hunger to taste Falcon and have him in his mouth, he kept it slow and kissed down to his hipbone almost casually.

"Motherfucker," Falcon muttered into his fist when Blane avoided the base of his cock to kiss his thigh instead.

Blane chuckled deeply. "You're fucking turned on already," he murmured. Falcon's dick was flushed pink and throbbing, and the head was glossy with precome already.

"Of course I am," Falcon grumbled. "Hurry up."

"And?"

"Suck me," Falcon mumbled, almost too quietly for him to hear.

"What—"

"*Suck me off,*" Falcon hissed, loud and clear. His hands tangled in Blane's hair, pushing his head toward his cock. "I need you. I need it."

Blane kissed open-mouthed and firmly, flicking his tongue along the skin from base to tip of the shaft, then swallowed it in one slow, smooth motion.

Falcon tasted as good as before, his shaft as velvety and firm and pleasing on the tongue. And like before, he squirmed and pushed his hips off the bed. "Jesus. Yes. *Yes, please. So good...!*"

Blane guided Falcon's hands to the bed, sucking tightly around the head and pushing his head down a few more times before pulling away.

Falcon gasped. "You—fuck—I need..."

"I know," Blane whispered, sliding up the bed to press a kiss against Falcon's throat. He made it obvious a moment later what he was doing as he pushed Falcon's knee aside and spread his stance, slotting his cock alongside Falcon's.

"Frottage?" Falcon breathed out. "Very old-fashioned. Greek."

Blane laughed breathlessly. "You can give me the history lesson later," he told him, reaching down to grip them both in one hand. He thrust slowly once or twice to get a feel for it, then braced himself firmly on one arm. He could already tell how goddamn good this was going to feel.

Falcon whimpered and grabbed Blane's shoulder blades, leaning up for another of those fierce, attention-grabbing, dirty kisses of his.

One thrust and stroke at a time, Blane squeezed them both firmly onward to the orgasms plunging toward them. The sensation of the ridges and firmness of Falcon against him was enough to bring him along, if the tightness of the ring of his fingers hadn't already been.

They were both so hot their skin glistened, bodies sliding together in easy heat.

Falcon was clearly on the edge, his fingernails digging into Blane's skin. He rolled his head away from the kiss to gasp for breath. "Fuck... Blane...!"

"Come on, baby," Blane whispered. "Don't hold out for me. Let go." To be honest, his world was already spinning, his muscles tightening until he couldn't breathe. He wasn't going to be able to stop himself for long, either.

As Falcon came, he arched into Blane's body, his arms looping around his back to press together tightly. His wetness spilled over Blane's fingers and cock, making him throb with extra need before he couldn't hold, either.

"Fuck. *Yes*," Blane groaned, throwing his head back. And then he was coming, too, thrusting hard against Falcon as they rode the wave of bliss together.

He let go at last, sticky and sweaty and feeling like he'd just run a marathon, but as he rolled onto his side, Falcon followed, keeping his arm around Blane.

Blane laughed under his breath and let Falcon cuddle into his chest, wiping his hand on his thigh and pulling him close even if he was overheating. "You good?"

"A little fucking more than good," Falcon mumbled into his chest, and Blane grinned even more.

"Was the teasing worth it?"

"Yeah. You can do *that* anytime," Falcon whispered.

"I was gonna finger you, too," Blane hummed. "But you were pretty easy. Maybe next time."

"Now I can't wait for next time. You calling me easy?" Falcon flicked Blane's nipple.

"Oof. Your orgasm was... easy to induce."

"No, that's dangerously close to vet territory," Falcon laughed. "That is not my kink."

Blane laughed richly, then kissed the top of Falcon's head before pulling back again. "Having your needs taken care of by a medical professional? I think you just did."

"I... shut up," Falcon laughed, rolling onto his back. "Oh, man. We're a mess."

"Totally worth it." Contentment was sinking into Blane's

bones, dragging on his eyelids. It wasn't even that late in the evening, but he wanted to nap already.

"Totally," Falcon whispered.

They lay together, shoulders nestled together, for another couple minutes, the silence between them not uncomfortable.

Finally, the inevitable: Falcon pushed himself upright. "I better... clean up. And get going, I suppose. Work and all. Wait, am I stranding you?"

"I got a coworker nearby who'll give me a lift," Blane shook his head with a smile at Falcon's thoughtfulness.

The next few minutes passed in a blur, and it wasn't until Blane was back in bed—alone this time—that it really sank in.

I want to do this again. And it sounded like Falcon wanted a next time, too. *Maybe, even if he doesn't want to date me... he'll let me stay around. Eventually I might win him over. Oh, God, don't think like that.*

He dragged a pillow over his face and then rolled over onto it. It was stupid to get his hopes up, especially when Falcon had hinted before that he didn't date. He wasn't going to magically change the guy's mind.

Blane couldn't keep on assuming without asking, but if he asked and got turned down, he might ruin this one good thing that finally felt like it might be within his grasp.

Rock and a hard place.

He fell asleep remembering the warmth and weight of Falcon against him.

CHAPTER

Thirteen

FALCON

FALCON TAPPED HIS FINGERS ON THE STEERING WHEEL IN TIME to the radio without noticing what song was playing.

It had been so long since he'd even seen Spencer—somehow, in a city this size, he'd managed to never run into him randomly. Maybe Spencer had been living elsewhere. Falcon hoped he still did.

Once he found a parking spot and the Starbucks they'd agreed to meet in, he locked his car, drew a breath, and walked in.

No sign of Spencer yet. Of course not—it was five to two, and Spencer was never early for anything. Falcon headed for the counter to buy himself a drink. He'd deliberately arrived early so he could get his own drink and his own table, and not have Spencer try to buy his favors.

Falcon chose a table on the end so he could walk away anytime and sat with his back to the wall so he could watch the door. Not that it was hard to miss Spencer's entrance.

"Look who it is!" His voice echoed around the place like it

did when he was trying to be a straight buddy meeting his straight buddy for some straight coffee.

"Hey." Falcon refused to rise to his feet for a hug, even though Spencer held out his arms. He was in some well-fitted slacks and shirt, probably taking a lunch break from his nice corporate lawyer's office job. The gesture looked sincere, but Falcon knew better than to let Spencer get close enough that he could avoid apologizing.

It forced Spencer to turn it into a grand gesture instead, before he waved at the counter. "I'd better get a drink. Can I get you anything?"

"I'm fine."

It gave him a chance to inspect Spencer's face, watch the way he acted. He was older now—of course. Both of them were. But he didn't act much older, because he still pushed past another customer to get into line first.

When he returned, Falcon let Spencer break the silence first. "So, uh, you're looking good," Spencer finally came out with.

"I know."

Spencer opened his mouth for a second, too taken aback to answer, and Falcon resisted the urge to laugh. "Uh." He seemed to try to brush it off. "Good to be together again. All this time. Jeez, it seems like yesterday."

"Seems like years ago to me," Falcon answered. He kept his tone light, even if he wanted to be pissed off. It was clear Spencer was trying to avoid the apology he'd implied this meeting was about.

"Too long," Spencer immediately said and nodded. "You're right."

Asshole. "That's not what I said," Falcon half-smiled and

leaned back in his seat, cradling his coffee cup by his chest between sips. "What are you here to tell me?"

Spencer drummed his fingers on the table. "Just to see you before the whole… you know, public sees us."

"My family?" Falcon laughed. "Not exactly the whole town."

"Yeah, yeah. I know." Spencer scanned his face, then leaned in. "I had an idea. You know? We could… go to the wedding together."

Falcon nearly reeled, but he managed to keep his composure. "*Now* you want me to?"

"Yeah. Yeah, that'd be fun. Just a date, no pressure. Drinks, dancing… you never know," Spencer winked.

Don't eviscerate him. Save it for the canvas. Falcon tilted his head. "Thanks for the offer. No."

"Isn't that what you always wanted?"

Falcon rose to his feet, leaving his cup behind. The bitter taste in his mouth didn't need any chasers. "You haven't changed a bit."

"Thanks."

"That's not a good thing. See you at the wedding, Spencer."

He barely managed to make it out the door before Spencer could call him back. His blood was pumping, his fingers curled into fists.

How long had he lasted? Five minutes? *Longer than Spencer used to last,* the mean voice at the back of his head added.

The thought made Falcon grin, relaxing enough to dig his keys out of his pocket. He drove on autopilot, his brain still turning over the meeting.

Stupid of him to go. *Stupid* to think Spencer might have

changed. *Stupid* to even accept an apology from him. *Stupid* to expect one.

Halfway through driving home, he had to pull over when his phone went off. If this was Spencer, he was gonna…

It was his sister.

How had his life suddenly become like a soap opera, where he had to check the caller ID before he answered?

"Hey," Rosalina greeted warmly. "This is your weekly wedding update! Is now a good time?"

"It's—uh, it's fine," Falcon quickly answered, pulling his thoughts away from *that* asshole.

"I just had to check that you're still okay arriving early to help with the setup. Are you?"

Falcon smiled to himself. "Yeah, of course! I promised. Not gonna let my big sis down."

"You're my favorite little brother," Rosalina answered, making them both laugh. "And the smartest, and the most handsome…"

"What else do you need me to do?"

Rosalina snorted. "Like I have to have an ulterior motive to compliment my little bro. But also, I might have screwed something up."

Uh oh. Falcon's mental phone book immediately opened. Did she need help with a printer? Florist? Caterer? He probably knew someone who knew someone… "What happened?"

"Spencer asked for your number."

Everything screeched to a halt. Years of practice—casual blankness, or a one-shouldered shrug in response to Spencer's name—kicked in again. "Huh?"

"C'mon. *Spencer.* You guys used to be best buddies." Rosalina wasn't letting him get away with it.

Falcon blew out a sigh. "Yeah. Right. Him."

"Well, uh… I remembered the fight… but you never told us much about it back then. I invited him before I thought about it. And then he has your number now. I'm an idiot. I *really* should have thought about that," Rosalina breathed out. "I'm sorry."

"No, no," Falcon assured her. "We're adults. We can handle it." *At least, I am. Maybe. Is wanting to show off that I'm happy and I've moved on and I've got a great life—even if I don't, even if I'm asking Blane to fake it—very adult?*

"Do you think you could make up?"

"No. He was always kind of a jerk," Falcon said bluntly. "Even though you were friends…"

"Yeah, he was," Rosalina agreed with a quiet laugh. "We just sort of fell into step. Then I guess I kept being friends with him because you were."

Falcon winced. *And he kept seeing me because you were.* "Anyway, nah. I'm still… well, he still doesn't respect me."

"The whole creative professional thing?" It was a convenient excuse, because it was true. If not the whole truth. He'd told Rosalina that Spencer told him to go into a real job when he decided to go to art school—which was true.

"Do you want me to uninvite him? Cause dude, I totally will. You know I will."

Falcon grinned to himself. His sister had always had his back. Given the chance back then, she probably would have, too. It was a nice feeling, to know his big sister was ready to do that.

But as sweet as the offer was, his gut instinct told him to turn it down. Getting Spencer uninvited wouldn't solve anything. The vindictive, petty side of him told him *yes*, and he didn't trust that impulse. Besides, this was a chance to not just show Spencer how far he'd come, but show himself. Even if he had further left to go.

And maybe... maybe... a genuine date.

It was a huge risk, asking Blane to a family wedding when they were so newly-dating. If someone asked that of him, he'd be surprised. But either way, he had to figure things out, and the best way out was through.

No. He wouldn't avoid Spencer. He'd face him like an adult, and he'd show Spencer exactly what he'd missed out on. Whatever the hell his game was—wanting to openly date *now*, at his sister's wedding, after years of secrecy and para-noia—Falcon wanted no part of it.

"No, but thanks. I'll just ignore him. Besides, I don't want to cause drama. I don't wanna have to uninvite my plus-one."

Rosalina gasped. *"Falcon.* Who is it? Tell me."

"Nope."

"You're such an ass. Tell me."

"Nope!" Falcon laughed. "Wait and see. Need anything else?"

Rosalina sighed dramatically. "I guess not. Ugh. Patience is not my strong suit."

"I don't think it suits anyone in this family," Falcon grinned. "Talk to you soon."

As he hung up, Falcon pressed his hand into his forehead. *What was I thinking? Crap. Now I have to show up with a date. Which means I have to ask him.*

CHAPTER
Fourteen

BLANE

Just lion in bed being lazy. Wish you were here. xox

Blane was glad the first thing he'd done on his lunch break was grab his phone, in case Falcon had texted.

It was gonna be a good lunch break. Blane grinned to himself and settled at the staff room table with his sandwich and his phone. Normally he might sit outside, but he'd spent the morning in the sunshine helping Gregory with checkups on the big cats, and then feeding animals. By the time his own lunch break came around, he was ready for shade and air conditioning.

"What's so funny?"

Gregory's voice made him jump as he started composing a text. He nearly hit *Send* too early. "Jesus! A little warning."

"Sorry," Gregory laughed as he let the door close and headed for the fridge. "But you look like the cat who got the cream."

"Or the lion," Blane murmured under his breath as he composed a text.

We all need a snail's pace day sometimes.

"You're texting that guy, aren't you? The one you went home with." Gregory smirked. "Is it a thing yet?"

"What do you mean a thing?" Blane busied himself unwrapping his sandwich so he didn't have to look at Gregory, but the back of his neck and ears were turning hot.

"You know. Official."

Falcon's response arrived: *After my whale of a day yesterday, I'm treating myself.*

"That sounds like commitment," Blane waved his hand, crunching on a carrot.

Gregory eyed him with another smirk. "Ah, and you don't like that."

"Fuck off."

"I'm not criticizing. It's nice to see you grinning like a loon."

"Thanks." Blane meant for the pun, as he made a mental note of it, but also... well, for caring. As coworkers went, Gregory was pretty ideal. They shared rides sometimes, duties at work sometimes. He worked as hard as Blane and didn't slack on Friday afternoons, and most importantly, he cared as much about the animals as Blane did.

"All power to you and whatever, but I'm going to eat outside so I don't have to watch you giggling over your phone."

Blane flipped him off, but once he was alone, his attention was quickly glued to the screen again.

Anything I can help with, or should I leave it a loon?

A dubious pun but I'll let it goat.

Blane choked. *That was even whorse.*

Did you just call me...?

Blane dropped his sandwich on the wrapper. *No! Of course not.*

He should have known Falcon was teasing, but he got his answer instantly: *You're cute when you're worried. Hahahahaha. Anyway I have a redikdikulous idea...*

Blane rolled his eyes and stuffed the rest of his sandwich in his mouth while he waited for Falcon to type.

So remember my ex coming to the wedding?

That was a good start. Blane raised a brow, then answered, *Yeah?*

He wanted to meet and apologize except he didn't. He just... basically propositioned me.

Hardly even conscious of his own reaction, Blane resisted the urge to bare his teeth. It was the most primal form of aggression an animal could show—motivated by fear, territorial disputes, or sometimes the urge to protect.

Which was it this time?

Falcon quickly texted again. *Obviously I walked out on him lol. But I kind of want to... there's no good way to ask this.*

What is it? Blane dipped his carrot sticks in hummus, one at a time, waiting for an answer. He got halfway through the container before he had a little wall of text to read all at once.

Would you be my plus-one and act like my new boyfriend for the wedding? I know it's kind of early to do a real "meet the family" thing, but I don't want to face him alone. And I'm showing my ugly side here, but I want to make him see what he missed out on, kwim?

Blane grinned to himself. The number of assholes he'd been on dates with who had been rude to him, or ghosted him, or ditched him halfway through dinner for their phone or for another guy at a club? The dating world was rough. He totally understood that reaction.

Besides... he was insanely attracted to Falcon despite Falcon's reluctance to commit, and he wanted to find out where that was coming from. If he could figure out if it was just a lack of interest or if there was something he could help with…

It was stupid to get his hopes up, he told himself again. Even stupider to keep making these assumptions about what Falcon wanted. He had never outright said *no*, but the idea that he might had stopped Blane from asking.

But seeing people around their exes or their families tended to explain so much about them. This gave him the chance to find out what kind of man Falcon was, and whether he had a hope's chance in hell of a future.

And, most importantly, whether Falcon was likely to say yes or no if he ever *did* get brave enough to ask.

So I go, show you off, make this asshole jealous, and get to meet your family? Sounds like a blast.

Really? It's not too weird?

Dude, it's like a movie plot. I can pretend I'm a high-class escort. Or a low-class one if you prefer ;)

OMG. But despite the response, Blane knew Falcon was laughing. A moment later, Falcon texted again. *Okay, you're a lifesaver. I also might have told my sister I was bringing a +1 and she's desperate for me to bring a man so she can say she knew all along... lol.*

Blane chose his words carefully. *I'm glad I'm the first man you thought of ;)*

I'm glad you said yes! God knows what I would have done without a date. Faked pneumonia?

Blane checked his phone, wincing when he saw he only had a couple minutes left of his break. *That's hard to fake. Go for a pinched nerve or something. Then you just can't get out of bed... and I can keep you company. But I forgot, you don't like that scenario...*

Falcon answered pretty quickly. *Now that you've described it, I could be interested ;)*

Enough to get to the zoo today?

Tomorrow? Falcon suggested. *And I can give you the wedding details.*

Deal. Tomorrow it is. Better get back to work.

Blane reluctantly threw away his trash and put his phone in his locker. It went off one more time before he could close it, so he flipped the screen up for a look.

XOX

He smiled to himself, then set it down again and closed his locker door, whistling as he strode out the door.

CHAPTER

Fifteen

FALCON

T HE ZOO WAS ALMOST A SECOND HOME BY NOW. H E FELT LIKE he'd been there more than anywhere else lately, but every time he walked through the gates, the same excitement flared up.

Falcon had a job to do today, but in his imagination, he was following Blane around at work. For research purposes, of course—to see the animals up close.

"Morning," he greeted the girl behind the counter at the closest snack station to the meerkat exhibit—Lacy.

After several visits, embarrassingly, Lacy was starting to recognize him. She'd commented on his collapsible easel and struck up a conversation about art last time.

"Back again?"

"I am. So are you, I see," he joked, scanning the menu. Of course he wanted coffee. It was going to be a long day of work. "Just a coffee, please."

"Giving up on painting, then?" Lacy retorted as she poured a cup from the pot, gesturing at the camera dangling from his wrist.

"Oh! No." He laughed. "I did a lot of quick sketches last week. Now I'm getting photo references."

"Right. It's gotta be hard to find anatomy references of specific things online sometimes."

"Yeah. There's books out there, but they cost like a thousand dollars," he snorted, rolling his eyes.

Lacy nodded. "I remember that much." She'd said last time that she'd used to sketch, but gave up over time. It always made Falcon sad to hear about that—so many people thought they were no good and stopped just when they could be making a breakthrough in technical details or style.

"Seriously, if art supplies didn't cost so much, artists wouldn't be so broke." Falcon rolled his eyes and handed over change, but his eye was drawn by movement. Two men walked past, in distinctive uniforms. Blane and Gregory.

Falcon resisted the urge to call out to them—Blane would see him soon, he was sure. The zoo wasn't that big.

"Photo references of what?"

Falcon turned red, realizing he was staring after the men. He *had* accidentally gotten Blane in a few shots last week. *Accidentally.* On accident. "Uh, different... animals."

"Sure," Lacy winked, sliding the cup over the counter and taking the change he handed her. "I heard them..." She trailed off, biting her tongue but smiling mischievously.

"Heard what?" Falcon couldn't resist asking.

"Oh, just them talking. Gregory was teasing Blane about you over lunch last week."

"So I know where to go for all the hot zoo gossip," Falcon laughed, his cheeks hotter than the cup in his hand.

"Honestly, they forget how their voices carry." Lacy winked. "Go get 'em, tiger."

Falcon raised his other hand and waved, still laughing

under his breath as he followed—*didn't* follow, happened to walk in the same direction as—the vets.

They had already disappeared into the staff area of the meerkat exhibit, so Falcon casually chose a spot by the Plexiglass where he was out of the way of the kids' viewing spot but still had a good line of sight to most of the exhibit.

He liked this zoo for more than Blane's presence. Although parts of it looked shabby—faded signs or paint that needed to be touched up—the animals were clearly kept with care. Now he knew why: people like Blane were there.

Falcon set his bag by his feet, then crouched by the glass to take some shots of the meerkats.

One was scurrying around near the glass, watching the visitors as much as it was being watched. Another couple seemed to be herding a group of smaller meerkats—pups, he assumed. What were babies called? Kittens? That seemed to suit their name better. He'd have to ask Blane.

The door opened and Blane entered. Falcon blushed again, but he took photos as Blane set down full food dishes, then retreated as curious meerkats popped up to scurry toward them from all over the sandy, rocky terrain.

It was cute to watch them eat, and very informative. Falcon snapped photos of the way they dexterously handled the food.

He was partway through a few initial sketches of zoo animals, but he was starting to feel like meerkats were a good direction to go for a series of their own. A lot of people found them cute, judging by the visitor flow in this area of the park. And Rosalina and Jenny could have the original first-in-series.

Falcon thought over the idea of doing a cartoon series for his other artist identity, too. It made sense to do multiple pieces on one subject while he had the references fresh in his mind. And he could already see the possibilities for messages about family, support, or sharing with groups of meerkats behind the text.

He was so distracted thumb-pecking ideas into his phone that he didn't see Gregory come up beside him until Blane's coworker spoke.

"We'll have to call you the meerkat man."

"Jesus." Falcon jumped, then breathily laughed. "I like them. They're cute."

"And the guy with them isn't bad, either," Gregory added with a smirk. When Falcon cast him a questioning glance, he said, "Oh, I'm straight... and I wouldn't date a coworker anyway. But Blane can't stay away from wherever you're working when you're here."

Falcon mumbled something and shrugged, not wanting to out him. He was pretty sure Blane had said he was out, but...

"It's cool. He said you two have a hot date tonight."

"He did?" Falcon grinned, his anxiety lessening. *How hot does he mean? I hope he means what I think.*

"I'm sure he mentioned it, yeah. And that he might need to be picked up tomorrow morning, again. Once or five times."

Blane was walking toward them now, empty dishes in his hands and a suspicious look on his face as he eyed Gregory. "Are you corrupting his innocent ears?"

Falcon laughed before he could stop himself, then cleared his throat. "Ah. My innocent ears. Yes."

Gregory cracked up. "I think it's the other way around. Okay, I gotta go deal with the big cats. You coming?"

"In a minute," Blane promised, handing over the dishes.

Falcon caught the teasing eye-roll Gregory gave Blane before he raised a hand in a wave and left.

Blane dusted his hands off, then slid them into the pockets of his coat. "You're here early. Staying the day?"

"I hope to. If I have someone to stay for."

"I can think of someone who hopes you are," Blane retorted playfully. He didn't get too close, but Falcon could respect that. He was at work, after all.

"Gregory said you were hoping to catch a ride tomorrow morning," Falcon teased.

Blane's grin was unrepentant. "If you insist on bugging me like this… distracting me at work…"

"Someone should. You're less grumpy after I've had my way with you." Falcon winked. "Better go help your buddy. I'll be around."

"Oh, I'll find you." It was said in an undertone, but with a playful little growl that made Falcon shiver with pleasure.

"I can't wait."

Once Blane walked off, Falcon stole a moment to look after him, then tried to focus his thoughts again. *References. Right. I was here for a reason.*

It was gonna be a long damn day.

"Now I see why you pack your own lunch," Falcon told Blane as he glanced at the red light, then his passenger.

"The burgers really aren't bad. Your mistake for not following my menu recommendations," Blane told him, his arms folded.

Falcon resisted the urge to laugh. "Zoo food sucks."

"Not all of it."

"Mmm." Getting him defensive was kind of fun. "The coffee isn't the best, either."

"It gets the job done."

"You know what else gets the job done?" Falcon made it very clear what he meant, slowing down the syllables and flashing a quick sideways glance.

The day had been hell, holding back from talking to Blane every time he saw him. He'd disappeared for a while to do more veterinary duties before reappearing to help with zookeeper tasks and a guided talk toward the end of the day.

Falcon resisted the urge to check that he still had his camera and all its precious images of the exhibits—sometimes with Blane around or in them.

"I have a few ideas," Blane murmured. He was looking at Falcon and not glancing away, and it took all Falcon's concentration to keep his eyes on the road. "A lot, in fact."

"Whatever we don't get around to, we can save for another night," Falcon promised with another quick wink.

"I like the way you think."

We're still keeping going, then. Good. Falcon was relieved their last encounter hadn't seemed to slow them down at all. In fact, Blane seemed more eager to spend time around him.

He wasn't really sure how to handle it. He'd long since healed from the feeling of being unwanted by Spencer except for sex, and he'd come to terms with the idea that he was worth being around, but he'd never really put it into practice.

It was all so... *easy.* It was hard not to be on guard because of that.

"Ah, here we go, right?" Falcon pulled up into Blane's driveway.

"You learn fast. You'll be coming over all the time now."

"Is that an offer?"

Blane glanced at him, and his voice was a bit more serious than Falcon expected when he said, "It might be."

Then he got out of the car, leading Falcon inside while Falcon's brain churned over that one.

Blane *cooked*.

How rare was a man who had a good job, friends and a life of his own, and cooked? Falcon tried his best to stop matching Blane up to the mental boyfriend list, but it was always hard when they were alone together.

"Supper was great," he said again as he loaded his dishes into the dishwasher. "Thanks."

It was simple—chicken and rice—but it did the job.

And it gave them a little while to hang out in the kitchen, talking about Blane's day at work and Falcon's current works in progress, and their families, and their favorite meals…

But the tension was impossible to ignore. Every time they brushed hands while cleaning up after supper, every lingering look across the table as they ate, it all built up under Falcon's skin.

He almost squirmed with impatience as Blane settled on the couch and gestured for him to join him.

"I'm glad you came over," Blane said, his voice soft.

Falcon sank into the comfy couch next to him and leaned in while Blane wrapped his arm around his shoulders. It was odd but cozy, and he… he liked it.

A simple touch on his bicep, the weight of an arm across his shoulders and neck, had him on edge, too. The comfort and arousal conflicted, making his brain not sure which direction it wanted to go more.

Oh. That's new. I want to cuddle first. Falcon drew a breath and let it go, resting his head on Blane's shoulder. "I'm glad, too. This is nice."

"Mmm." Blane leaned in to kiss his cheek, his breath warm, and Falcon's dick made up his mind.

A quiet noise escaped as Blane squeezed him into him.

"You're on edge," Blane observed, his voice low and teasing.

Falcon rolled his head back. "And you know exactly what you're doing."

"I have some idea, yes." Blane's finger played with the sleeve of Falcon's t-shirt, trailing along bare skin. "You could hardly sit still during supper."

"I… I'm really into you."

"You want to be even more into me? Or vice versa, Mr. Vers?" Blane grinned.

Oh my god, he means... "Really?"

"Is it too soon?" Blane sounded concerned, his finger stopping.

"*Fuck*, no," Falcon laughed. "I like blowjobs, but with the right guy…"

"And that's me?" Blane leaned in, his lips warm as he mouthed the edge of Falcon's jaw. "I'm glad. Anal isn't a requirement for me, per se, but it can feel great."

"Yeah, it can." Falcon moaned and tipped his head so Blane could kiss his ear and neck. His nails dug into Blane's thigh with the self-control it took not to grab him and ride him until dawn.

"You're gorgeous," Blane whispered. "You know that, right?"

Falcon nodded. "Most guys don't like that I do."

Blane laughed abruptly. "No? They wanna be the only

one that tells you that? Fuck it. I hope everyone tells you you are."

Holy shit. Falcon was blushing so hard he wanted to curl up and wait for Blane to stop looking at him. He turned his face away, but Blane cupped his cheek gently, pulling his face back toward him to kiss him on the lips.

The kiss was deep and firm, strong. The kind of kiss Falcon could—and did—melt into. He closed his eyes and sighed unconsciously, his lips parting so Blane could slide his tongue between them, then suck his lower lip between his.

It was nice to give in and let Blane *have* him. In theory, anyway. Blane was going slowly, one hand still resting halfway up his thigh, maddeningly far away from his most sensitive skin.

"Nnnh," he groaned sharply in frustration, making Blane chuckle.

Blane murmured into his ear, "Impatient, are we?" He lipped the earlobe.

"Not all of us have that stoic Spartan shit going on," Falcon grumbled, trembling with pleasure at the nerves that lit up in his body.

"Now who's grumpy?"

Falcon snorted. "Shut up and… do something."

"Oh, I'm doing things." Blane licked the rim of his ear slowly, running his tongue all the way around the edge to the lobe, until Falcon's skin was on fire, his nails pressing hard into Blane's thigh and the couch. "And there's so much left to do."

Blane moved swiftly when he finally did, pushing Falcon flat onto his back along the couch and straddling him. He pulled his t-shirt slowly up, dipping his head down to kiss the bare stomach he revealed.

"Fuck," Falcon hissed. The sudden warm, wet heat so close to his aching cock made his hips jerk up, but he was trapped by the weight of Blane.

Blane kissed again and again as he pulled the t-shirt up, way too slowly for Falcon's liking, covering every inch of skin between his navel and collarbone.

He took particular care, when it was bunched around Falcon's neck, to kiss each nipple.

"Fuck fuck fuck," Falcon mumbled, arching deliberately this time to grind against Blane. He needed some stimulation —something—or he was gonna go crazy.

"Hold still," Blane ordered. "If you're patient, I'll get around to it."

Falcon trembled on the edge of obedience and disobedience, wondering which option would be more fun—which would bring them both more pleasure.

In the end, he reluctantly flattened himself on the couch again, letting his cock throb without relief in his jeans. "Better be worth it," he mumbled.

"I promise," Blane whispered. He pulled the shirt over Falcon's head, then up his forearms to his wrists, and left it there.

"Oooh." Falcon grinned, another flash of heat running through his body as Blane twisted the fabric a couple times and looped it over his fists. It wasn't so tight he couldn't easily get free, but the *idea* was thrilling.

"Patience," Blane murmured again, pressing his lips in a long, slow kiss that gentled the sharp-edged need running through Falcon's veins.

I've never felt like this before from... just foreplay. That said, Falcon couldn't remember anyone taking this kind of time in foreplay, or being this good at it. First dates weren't conducive to it—more awkward fumbling, or straight to fucking.

But Blane seemed determined to unwrap him slowly, like a gift, and unravel his self-control along the way.

Blane's lips were on his collarbone now, then his nipple. Warm, wet, *good*. Falcon panted for breath as Blane sucked and pinched the nubs and the skin around with his lips.

"Blane," he moaned quietly. "You're fucking good."

He wanted to touch, but he kept his hands above his head, stretching himself out in an invitation for Blane to have him whenever he wanted.

Finally, Blane's lips were working back down the center of his body all the way to his waistband, his hands fumbling at the button.

"It's hard to do this when you're squirming," Blane laughed.

Falcon blushed. "Can't help it. My balls are fucking blue by now."

"Bet they aren't," Blane murmured. "Or if they are, I can warm them up again..."

Falcon tried to stifle his gasp at the thought of his sensitive skin in Blane's gentle mouth, but it didn't work.

Blane chuckled deeply and pulled his jeans and underwear down. Just like before, he left them around his ankles.

"You *are* kinky." Falcon smirked up at him, his cock finally—mercifully—free, but in need of stimulation, stat.

Blane winked. "If you want me to be."

"I do if *you* want *me* to be."

"We'll talk, then," Blane grinned. "But I have better plans."

"Like wha—uhhhht," Falcon tried to finish the word without losing his dignity and lost the battle. The hot, wet mouth around the tip of his cock all of a sudden was almost too much, and he gritted his teeth as his whole body throbbed with the tingly charge of need.

Blane sucked him in to the base of his cock, then pulled his mouth up again, bobbing his head slowly but keeping the suction tight.

His thighs almost shook with the force building up in his body. They were tight, and so was his stomach. He could hardly move if he wanted to now, except for the desire to fuck Blane's mouth hard and fast.

But the knowledge that Blane had plans—and had him tied up, in a way—made him stop. Falcon curled his toes into the couch, gasping with desperation when Blane pulled his mouth off him.

"Is this the fucking? Please fuck me," Falcon groaned, rubbing his body against Blane's and trying to hook a leg around his waist.

"Upstairs."

Falcon didn't even try to make his whine more graceful. "*Blane.*"

"C'mon." Blane gently untangled him from his clothes and left them on the couch, then took his hand and tugged him to his feet.

Falcon ground against Blane as soon as they were standing. "A wall? A floor?"

"An extra ten seconds and you can have lube."

"Don't fucking care," Falcon muttered, but he grinned. "Fine."

"Up you get." Blane scooped him off his feet, and Falcon gasped, wrapping his legs around his waist.

"You aren't—carrying me upstairs? You ridiculous man," Falcon laughed as Blane started to make for the stairs. "I *can* walk."

"I said I'd take care of you." Blane's voice was teasing. "Your knees are all wobbly. You might fall."

"*You* might fall," Falcon retorted, but he buried his face in Blane's shoulder as the ground lifted away from him and the stairs began.

"Not if you don't distract me."

Of course Falcon wasn't going to let that go. He freed one arm from Blane's neck and reached between them until he had both their dicks lined up against each other and squeezed together.

"Little fucker," Blane whispered, his voice hoarse, when Falcon stroked slowly, casually.

"I gotta make my own fun here."

"Oh, I *promise* you don't," Blane growled right into his ear, and suddenly he was on the bed, Blane over him and grinding hard.

Falcon moaned and gave in, letting his arms fall above his head while Blane rutted against him until his damp cock started to pulse with the same need that he'd just barely avoided downstairs.

"Fuck me. Now," Falcon panted. He ached for something in him—not just anything, but Blane. He wanted *all* of his senses to be filled with the strong certainty of him.

Wet fingers touched him as Blane pulled away, and Falcon eagerly spread his legs, gulping back his gasp at the cool gel against needy nerves.

Two fingers slid slowly into him, deep enough to rub the sensitive nerves on the way in and out. Then Blane's cock head was against him, hot, rounded, and huge. Falcon pushed up and into him as he breathed out.

He was inside, filling Falcon up with the kind of heat he'd dreamed of since they first bumped into each other.

Falcon's eyes fluttered open, and he caught Blane watching him closely, with something... something fond in his expression.

His heart fluttered. The look didn't vanish when he looked straight at him. "You all right?"

"Yeah," Falcon whispered. "More than."

Like they'd agreed, casual anal wasn't always all it was cracked up to be, but this... this wasn't walking into a guy's house and finding himself bent over the table two minutes later.

It wasn't coaxing himself into arousal and excitement, it was just the opposite—trying to hold back on the passion Blane had ignited under his skin.

Falcon *needed* him.

Blane filled him up in slow, steady thrusts until he bottomed out. His cock felt like Falcon's utter limit, but in the best possible way. That expression was serious. "Still good?"

"Fuck, yes," Falcon hissed with impatience. "You have a big cock, I have big dildos. I'm good."

Blane's laugh was *beautiful*. Startled from him, there was no restraint, no half-checking to see if anyone was watching. It was a kind of joy that sprang straight from the soul, and Falcon couldn't help but stare at his expression—the tiny crinkles in the corners of his eyes, the flash of so many teeth.

"I love your attitude."

Falcon flushed with pleasure but tried to play it cool. "Yeah, yeah. Show me what you got."

And Blane did, with thrusts that took away Falcon's capacity to be his usual perky, incorrigible self. He didn't take it easy, either, setting just the right pace.

Shit, he was in amazing shape. Blane's muscles rippled as

he braced himself on his forearms, his ass flexing and thighs tightening with each hard thrust delivered at just the right angle into Falcon's needy tightness.

Falcon realized he was panting, "Fuck," and, "Yes!" under his breath and rolled his head back, clearing his throat to moan them louder.

Blane's flushed cheeks and intense eyes told him that he was getting close, if the demanding pace didn't. Good. The electric charge that rippled along Falcon's skin was going to be impossible to resist this time around.

"You're so good. Fucking *hot*," Falcon moaned, digging his nails into Blane's back and hauling him down to kiss him hard, open-mouthed, with tongue and teeth.

And Blane met him halfway, kissing dirty and panting into his mouth. "Gonna come in you, baby." The condom made that half-true, but Falcon still shivered with delight at the words.

"Yeah. I'm gonna, too," Falcon managed. "I'm so—so goddamn close. Gonna… Blane…"

It could be like this all the time. The thought sent shivers of agreement through Falcon, but he set it aside for later. No sense making rash statements—offers—when his brain was close to as primal as it had ever been.

Yes, yes. Yes, I want it to be. "Yes!" He arched against Blane, his thighs trembling and tightening as he spilled his wet need across himself.

Blane growled and redoubled his pace, fucking him until the bed creaked, and then he heard his name—breathless but unmistakable—and Blane crashed into him, thrusts erratic and deep.

When Blane's arms started to weaken, his cock soften, Falcon pulled Blane against him as he slid out of him. He didn't feel empty, though, with Blane right here above him, blanketing him with both his weight and the very energy of his presence. All he could smell or taste or think of was Blane.

Shit. Oh, shit. I love him.

It was too soon—too casual a relationship—not the right time—just the orgasm talking. Falcon's mind fumbled for excuses, but the truth was undeniable. He felt it in his heart more than his head.

Blane's breathing slowed, and he finally rolled onto his side slightly. "Am I crushing you?"

"I like crushes," he mumbled.

Blane chuckled slightly, running a finger up Falcon's side and shifting onto a forearm. "Good. It's easy, with you."

To crush on me? He has to mean that, doesn't he?

Falcon's mind fumbled for words, and the first thing he came out with was a half-panicked, "Are you still on for the wedding?"

Blane blinked a few times as if trying to figure him out. No wonder. Falcon didn't even know where that had come from himself, and he was blushing now, trying to think how to take back the words without sounding totally weird.

"Yeah, I am," Blane said, cutting off his thoughts with a confident little smile. "If you want me to be. A fake date?"

"Yeah," Falcon whispered, but his eyes caught Blane's and held them. The question there was met with his own.

Neither of them dared break the silence for a long minute. Then, Blane slowly smiled and leaned in to kiss Falcon for long enough that he'd nearly forgotten the question.

"It'll be fun."

Blane turned onto his back and pulled Falcon against his

chest in an easy motion, and Falcon let him. It gave him the chance to tuck his head against his chest and look down, not straight into his face. And recover himself.

And think about what had just been said—not said—in that moment.

"Yeah. Yeah, it will be."

CHAPTER
Sixteen
BLANE

"AND WHEN'S THE WEDDING?"

"This weekend." Falcon's elbows rested on the marble countertop of the breakfast bar, his chin on his fists.

Blane raised his eyebrows as he stirred the scrambled eggs with a wooden fork. "So soon? I feel like the backup prom date."

"No!" It was a bit hastier than Falcon meant, because he cleared his throat and rolled his shoulders the way he did when he was trying to be cool. "I was just… procrastinating on asking. Nervous. You know." He intently studied the rest of the kitchen around Blane.

Blane held back his smile. "Mmm. I see. Okay, eggs are ready."

"I can't believe you cook breakfast, too." Falcon pretended to swoon, and nearly slipped off his stool.

Blane jerked toward him, an arm out, then put his hand down when Falcon caught himself. "Don't break anything. I don't want to use my training on humans."

"And I don't want a cone of shame," Falcon laughed, settling himself again.

Blane put down the plates side by side. He'd already set the breakfast bar with placemats, utensils, and condiments. For a moment, he'd considered bringing one of the African violets from the living room in, but that had seemed a bit…

A bit too romantic? Especially after last night's unfinished business. *Take it slow. That's the name of the game.*

"I cook breakfast for myself on the weekends. If I get up early enough, during the week… but I usually don't," Blane smiled.

He'd awoken early this morning, his arm over Falcon, who was curled into a ball and tucked into his chest. It was an experience he wanted to repeat.

"I have coffee… and then coffee… and occasionally toast," Falcon countered.

Blane pulled a face. "How do you live until lunchtime?"

"I dunno. Air? Huffing paint fumes?" Falcon's lips twisted into a little smile. "Anyway, bon appetit."

"Merci," Blane chuckled. "Do you speak French?"

"Non, non," Falcon waved a hand and grinned. "Just a smattering. I did a summer abroad in France during my art degree."

"Oh, really?" Blane looked over at him. "How was it?"

"It was a two-month intensive course. I didn't actually see a lot, outside the art galleries and stuff, obviously. But I learned a ton."

Blane nodded. "I've never been to Europe. One day, maybe."

"Too many people say *one day, maybe,* to feel like they'll have an escape from the mundane nine-to-five. And they never *do* anything about it." Falcon's voice, passionate as always, was frustrated and tight. "They let themselves hold themselves back with *someday*, instead of making it a goal, making it reality."

Blane set down his fork and squeezed Falcon's forearm, his mind spinning. "I guess you're right." He'd never really *planned* to travel. On his vacations, he saw family or friends, or just stayed at home and caught up on housework. Money wasn't tight, but it probably cost less these days to travel than he thought. It was just the motivation that was missing. "It upsets you?"

Falcon gave him a quick, apologetic smile and looked over. "Sorry. That was a bit of a rant. Yeah…"

"No, it's okay. I like seeing you get passionate. I just don't like seeing you upset."

Falcon relaxed, smiled at him. "I don't know where that came from. Normally I take the *you can do it!* approach." He laughed under his breath.

"Stress. The wedding planning," Blane suggested.

"Maybe. And…" Falcon trailed off, then picked up his fork again and finished his eggs.

Blane let him have a minute before he prompted, "And… your ex?"

"Yeah. I was okay seeing him the other day—it didn't upset me. I'm way over it," Falcon laughed. "But he *is* annoying. And then I can't stop comparing…" he trailed off again, his gaze flickering to Blane.

Blane's cheeks flushed. *Are we doing this?* "It's natural to compare," he said.

"Mm." Falcon quickly looked at his plate. "Great breakfast. I like your cooking. I should take a turn."

"Do you? Cook, I mean?" That seemed a safer subject, since Falcon had taken the quickest 180 he could.

"Occasionally. Like I said, toast for breakfast. I'm pretty good at ramen, rice and beans, all the art student gourmet meals." Falcon grinned. "And eggs any which way."

"Do my eggs measure up?"

Falcon reached under the bar toward Blane's crotch. "Oh, yes."

Blane laughed and reflexively jerked away, then swatted at his hand. He nearly knocked over his orange juice. "Hey, you. Behave."

"You mean, don't get you all turned on before you have to go to work?" Falcon teased. "By the way, I can give you a ride. Spare you Gregory's tormenting for another few minutes."

"Would you mind?" Blane smiled.

"Not at all." Falcon seemed sincere about it. "The least I can do for you, after last night," he added, wiggling his eyebrows.

Blane snorted and elbowed Falcon, trying not to laugh with his mouth full. Once he swallowed, he managed to answer. "You're *trouble*."

"Am I?" Falcon raised his brows. "I hadn't noticed."

Blane cast him a skeptical look and finished his breakfast. As he carried the dishes to the dishwasher, Falcon found the downstairs bathroom and played with his hair, getting it sticking up just right. Blane bit back his amusement.

"Pretty enough to go?" he teased.

Falcon sauntered out and ran his hand through Blane's hair to muss it up. "I always am."

I think... I could get used to this. "What are you doing tonight?" Blane didn't want to sound too eager, but it felt natural to want to be around Falcon as much as possible.

Especially if he was going to make that asshole, Spencer, jealous.

"Not much of anything," Falcon answered playfully, leaning into him. "I could be persuaded to change those non-plans."

"How about I text you over lunch?" Blane suggested.

"Perfect. Come on, get to my car before I find other ways to distract you." Falcon grinned at him and led the way out of his house.

Blane took a moment to gaze after him before he pulled himself together. *Right. Work. That exists.*

When Falcon was around, it was all too easy to forget everything.

CHAPTER
Seventeen

FALCON

Shifting his grocery bag from one arm to the other to dig in his pocket for the keys, Falcon froze with his key halfway into the lock.

He was pretty sure he'd just heard something from *inside* the apartment. Then he questioned himself: why the hell would it be? It could have been a trick of his mind, or a noise from the downstairs neighbors, or anything.

There were two possibilities. Well, three. No, now that his brain was working on it, even more.

It probably wasn't a crazy art collector intending on chaining him in his basement. And if it was, maybe he was hot. With that thought firmly in mind, eyes narrowed in trepidation, he slowly turned the key the rest of the way and pushed the door open.

Human eyes really weren't designed to look around edges easily. People ought to have eye stalks, like snails.

"Oscar! What the fuck are *you* doing here?"

Falcon pushed the door the rest of the way open and pressed his hand over his chest with relief at the best possible option—not that he'd say no to a rich patron, as long as the chaining was optional. And if Blane didn't mind. The thought made him blush.

His best friend had been sprawled on the couch, but he leapt to his feet with the poise of a classically-trained dancer, ending up on tiptoe with his arms spread wide. Even hugging him felt like getting dragged into performance art, but Falcon crossed the floor in a few quick strides to sweep him into his arms.

They hugged tightly before Falcon let go and leaned back to inspect Oscar. "You look shitty. Did you just get in?"

"Really late last night. I figured I'd surprise you. I hoped I wouldn't surprise you and your new boy toy." Oscar flashed a rueful grin. He'd given up his apartment to keep his costs lower, and he had spare keys to Falcon's place so he could crash when he was in town—which wasn't often these days.

"Luckily for you, we were at his place."

"Damn. I missed the show, didn't I?" Oscar's expression held wicked delight as Falcon's cheeks heated up.

"I'll tell you about him in a bit. What about you?"

Oscar waved his hand in a broad, sweeping motion and turned on his heel. "Coffee is preferable."

Well, that's never a good sign. "I'll start, then," Falcon offered, tailing him to the kitchen and hopping up onto the counter.

"Yes. Tell me. From the start."

It was harder than he'd thought to sum up this… *whatever this was…* between them. "Well, we met when I was at the zoo, sketching—oh my God, are you going to be in town this weekend for the wedding?" Falcon's voice rose.

"No, babe. I fly out Friday."

"Shit." Falcon playfully kicked him. "I never get you for more than a day!"

"I know, I know." Oscar patted his knee and rummaged for cups. "I'm sorry. I'm surprised they gave me this much time away."

"The money's gotta be good, though. Right?"

Oscar made a so-so gesture with his hand and grinned. "As good as I can expect at this stage. I'm not soloing or anything. And," he drawled, "back to you."

"Oh! So I was sketching, and I was in the way of the staff entrance. He was a little grumpy about it. I fell for him instantly." Falcon pretended to swoon.

Oscar gasped. "How romantic."

"He's one of those guys who likes animals more than people, but he has a group of close friends, too, so… he's not a total lone wolf weirdo."

"Like Spencer."

"Like Spencer," Falcon agreed, rolling his eyes. "Nothing like him, you'll be happy to know."

"And I get to meet him?"

"Yes! We're probably hanging out tonight."

Oscar gave him a crooked smile as he handed over a cup of coffee. "Oh, good. Third wheel again."

It only stirred Falcon's curiosity about what was going on in his friend's life, but he kept a lid on it for now. Oscar would only talk when *Oscar* was ready to talk. Until then, pushing him would get him nowhere. "If he wants to be my lover, he better get with my friends. Well. Friend."

That was a *little* overstating it. He knew plenty of people in the arts scene here, he just didn't devote enough time to maintaining friendships to call them close friends. Not like

Oscar, whom he could see in real life once in a blue moon and still pick up with every time like it was yesterday.

"I'll be happy to judge him. Scare him a little." Oscar took him by the hand to tow him over to the couch, then sat at an angle and cupped the mug between his hands. "So, you like him."

"Yeah." Falcon cleared his throat and studied a canvas nearby.

"But you don't know where you're going yet?"

"That's just it." Falcon sighed and scrunched his nose. "I was worried I was using him, but... he seems to be on board with this whole wedding fake-date idea. And there's moments when we look at each other, and..." he trailed off.

"What?"

It sounds crazy. Falcon shook his head and sipped his coffee, nearly spilling it down his shirt when Oscar nudged his knee. "Fine. It feels like he's the one. It's stupid, right? I hardly know him, but..."

"They always say when you meet the one, you'll know."

"It wasn't just chemistry." Falcon fell over himself to explain, setting his coffee mug almost untouched on the side table. "Like, yeah, the sex is hot, but... it's more than that. It's like we click. Being around him feels so easy. And it does with you too, but..." He fumbled for words.

Oscar shook his head. "No, no. I get it."

"Are you...?" Falcon poked his knee. "Gonna tell me?"

Oscar sighed. "Nothing to tell, really. There was a guy and now there's not."

"I'm sorry, babe." For a moment, Falcon felt guilty about gushing so much. "You'll find someone."

"Maybe after I'm retired."

"Aww. Don't talk like that," Falcon frowned.

"No, for real. I mean, dancers don't exactly have long careers," Oscar pointed out, his lips quirking into a smile. "I'm fine for another… what have I got? Ten years, if I make it that far? Five?"

"Okay, shut up. Now you're just moping," Falcon told him sternly.

Oscar smiled wryly. "Have you thought of being a dance teacher? Ruthless. I think it's the travel and sleep deprivation talking."

"Well, make them shut up." Falcon leaned over to glance out the window. "Sunny today. So I'm taking you for a good walk around downtown until you're cheerful again. How are your feet?"

"No worse than usual." Oscar laughed. "Nothing to show off, but I can walk."

"Okay, let's get your ass outside and soak up the Vitamin D, dude."

Falcon got the text a few minutes after lunchtime started. He was stretching out next to Oscar on the park bench as they ate crusty sandwiches and fended off pigeons. As soon as the phone buzzed in his pocket, it was in his hand.

"That was quick," Oscar teased.

"Shut up," Falcon mumbled as he read.

One of my pilot buddies is in town tonight before he flies out early tomorrow. I gotta see him while he's here. Want to meet him? No pressure.

Falcon smiled to himself. That was convenient. "Did you want to meet Blane? Sounds like he'll be bringing along a friend, so you can be third-wheels together," he teased.

"Yeah, sure," Oscar agreed. "I gotta meet this guy before you propose."

Falcon's jaw dropped and his cheeks flushed as he stared at his friends, thumbs hovering over the screen of his phone. "Dude!"

"What?" Oscar smirked. "You can't tell me you haven't thought about it."

Falcon stuck his middle finger up at Oscar and stared at his phone, trying to compose a text that made sense in return. He really didn't need *those* thoughts getting in the way.

Sounds great! My BFF is actually in town too! So, double date? ;)

It's a deal. I know this cute pizza place. Sound good?

Falcon laughed under his breath. *Do you really love pizza that much? What are you doing living in Tennessee, then?*

Who doesn't love pizza? Don't tell me you don't or it's off.

Falcon laughed again. *I do. Okay, see you when? 6?*

Perfect.

When Falcon looked up again, Oscar had his arms folded and a huge smirk on his face.

"Oh, shut *up*," Falcon growled playfully and shoved him. "I'm taking it slow."

"Are you boyfriends?"

"No, not even that. Depending on how the wedding goes..." Falcon trailed off.

Oscar tilted his head. "But you know he's the one?"

"Don't say it like *that*," Falcon grumbled, but his heart did a funny lurch. "I mean, if it doesn't work out, I'll let it go and... find someone else I click with that much. Eventually."

What he didn't say was how low his hopes were of that

ever happening. It had taken him almost a decade to find someone he was genuinely interested in and vice versa.

Oscar reached out to squeeze his knee. "It'll work out," he said with all the confidence Falcon wished he could muster up in himself. "If it means enough to you."

"Right. Let's get you home for a nap before tonight." He didn't want to wear his friend out in the precious little time he could take off his feet. Falcon offered Oscar his arm, but Oscar swatted it away with a laugh and pushed himself to his feet.

It does. He does. I want him to.

CHAPTER
Eighteen
BLANE

"Dude, how do you even stay alive?"

Roman laughed richly as he let the hotel room door close behind him. "Great question. As much sex and sleep as possible."

"I can see the use of at least one of those things," Blane chuckled, clapping Roman on the back as he hugged him tightly. A chance to see his buddy was always worth it, since he often went a month or two without being able to make it to one of their regular gatherings.

"If you don't see the use of both sleep and sex, you're not getting enough of one of them. Which is it?"

Blane flipped him off and let him lead the way into the elevator, then leaned against the bar inside. Roman always had nice hotels—that was the perk of being a pilot with as much status as him. Blane forgot Roman's explanations of it, because they tended to be laced with his own ego, and he was way too practiced at ignoring that.

"It's not sex," Roman grinned, leaning in. "You've been awfully quiet about that new boy toy."

"He's not a—" Blane started, then cut himself off and glared. He'd fallen right into Roman's trap.

Roman patted his cheek. "Awww."

Blane smacked his hand away and shoved him, then braced himself as Roman shoved back. Their brief tussle was brought to an end by the elevator slowing and arriving at the lobby, where they straightened themselves out and acted innocent strolling out of it.

Sometimes it still felt like high school when they got together, and he had to fight to remember that they were in this fancy-ass hotel because they had *careers* now.

"Anyway, yeah, don't scare him off." Blane glared at him. "Or hit on him."

Roman raised his hands. "I won't, man. It's good to see you getting involved with someone."

More so than anyone else, Blane thought Roman understood where he was coming from. Sex was great and all—and Roman was much more vocal about having it frequently with no strings—but they both craved the kind of affection and intimacy of letting their guard down with one person.

"Yeah. It's good to be," Blane admitted, stepping through the turning door of the hotel and leading Roman around the corner to the parking spot he'd finally found. In downtown Knoxville, it wasn't easy. And then there were the fucking assholes who didn't understand how to park, making it harder for everyone.

Blane managed to creep out of the parking spot he'd been almost jammed into within the mere fifteen minutes he'd been inside. Then it was off to the pizza place.

"Speaking of which," Blane mentioned once he wasn't fighting the urge to dent rude people's bumpers, "how about that boy in... Singapore?"

"Nah." Roman waved a hand in a now-familiar gesture that meant it had ended somehow—probably by him bringing up marriage a week in. Bless his heart, Roman simply didn't *get* why guys ran the other direction as fast as their feet could take him.

"Just, *nah?*" Blane chuckled. "Man, do what we're doing. Take it slow."

"Slow?" Roman snorted. "I'll believe it when I see it."

"Glacially. We aren't even together. We're fake-boyfriends for his sister's wedding this weekend."

Roman's eyebrows couldn't have climbed any higher.

"And we haven't brought up the word yet. Not really."

Roman was still silent.

"Oh, fuck off. We're almost there." Blane ignored Roman's skeptical look as he found parking, then led the way into the restaurant.

They were there before the other guys, so they grabbed a table and ordered tap water all around, then started flipping through the menus. Blane sat facing the door so he could see them arrive and wave them over.

It wasn't long before Falcon stepped inside, a tall and slender man walking beside him with the kind of poise he'd expect from a model. *Oh, man. Roman's in trouble.* Blane half-rose and waved them over.

"Blane Winters," Roman whispered. "You did *not* warn me."

Blane didn't have time to answer, so he just grinned at his friend. When Falcon arrived, he leaned down to peck Blane on the lips, then took the chair next to him. "Hey!"

"You made it," Blane greeted, his cheeks flushing at the look Roman was giving him. "So this is Roman. I'm Blane."

He shook hands with Falcon's friend. "Oscar," the man introduced himself, looking them both over.

Once the introductions were over, Blane found that Roman couldn't have beer for work reasons and Oscar declined, too. So he ordered a round of Cokes, and they all picked up the menus with that awkward shuffle.

With Roman there, though, it wouldn't be boring. After they ordered, he set his mind to conversation. "So, you're the artist?" He grinned at Falcon. "What do you draw?" He had a way of setting everyone around him at ease—when he wasn't trying to get into their pants.

"Whatever pays the bills," Falcon told him. "Lately, animals—hence our meeting," he glanced at Blane. "But I do cutesy cartoon merchandise online, and more serious gallery work. Nothing too high-concept, though. I like food."

Roman laughed. "Smart. I like the approach." Blane could tell he was already warming up. *Unemployed, my ass,* Blane thought.

Oscar stretched languidly, his glass in one hand as he listened in, but Roman wasn't about to let him sneak under the radar. "And you?" Roman addressed Oscar.

"I'm a dancer. It's much less sexy than it sounds."

Roman raised a brow. "How much less?"

"The flexibility is a perk," Oscar responded, making them all laugh. "But the rest of it?"

Roman grinned, and Blane could feel how much self-control it was taking him not to hit on him. "Is that your main job?"

"I'm lucky and young enough yet that it is," Oscar said with a nod and a frank smile. "But eventually I'll probably move into teaching."

"Huh." Roman nodded, looking back at Falcon. "And you two are friends?"

Oscar set down his glass. "Have been for a few years. We met at… was it your show?"

"No, someone else's," Falcon said. "I try to make it to everyone's events and vice versa. It's a nice little supportive community here."

"I like that. Aviation can be cutthroat," Roman admitted with a laugh. "Getting my current position wasn't easy. And now I have the least seniority of any captain my age—not that there are many—and no family, so they send me to do all the last-minute stuff. Lots of filling in."

Humble brag there, Blane observed, biting back his smile. He'd been wingman enough to know that Roman was fishing for interest from Oscar.

Falcon had been frowning for the last minute. He interrupted abruptly, "That must be stressful. Being on the road all the time. Hard to maintain relationships like that."

Roman straightened up and stretched, shrugging casually. "Yeah, it is hard sometimes."

"I've got some friends like that," Blane chimed in to cut the tension, nodding at Roman since he knew the guys he meant. "One's a musician. He was touring a lot until he met my buddy Nico. Had to revamp their whole lifestyles to make it work."

"It's going well for them, though." Roman smiled to himself. "It's cute to watch them. If… annoying. New couples. Ugh."

"I know," Oscar said, and Blane sensed he was just barely holding back a smirk. "They can't keep their eyes off each other."

"Fuck off," Falcon told Oscar, which made them all break out laughing again.

Blane squeezed Falcon's shoulder, then cheered as the garlic bread arrived.

It didn't take long before they'd torn it apart.

"So are your friends all getting paired off?" Roman asked Oscar.

"Yes! Oh, God. It's weird. I mean, it doesn't always last, but some of them are starting to, like, get married." Oscar pretended to shudder.

It took effort for Blane not to look pointedly at Roman.

Roman's foot landed on his as he laughed, would-be casually. "Yeah. Yeah, I know. At our age. Weird."

"Some of the guys in my company—two of them actually just got engaged," Oscar smiled. "And others have boyfriends back home. It's hard, though. On the road. I mean, probably not as hard as your job…"

"No, no. At least I usually get assigned to a particular region or routes, you know? When I'm not filling the gaps. So to speak," Roman smirked.

Blane groaned and Falcon and Oscar laughed.

"But do you go to the same cities much?" Roman was asking Oscar.

Blane leaned into Falcon. "I was worried they'd feel like the third wheels, you know," he murmured.

Falcon laid his arm along the back of Blane's chair after a glance around the restaurant. "I know what you mean. I was glad you brought a friend, too. I wanted you to meet Oscar, but yeah, that would have sucked."

Blane tried not to bristle as Oscar laid a hand on Roman's shoulder. *He's hiding it, but Roman's still hurting over that Singa-*

pore guy, knowing him. He itched to interrupt the rebound before it could happen.

"How was your day?" Falcon asked, distracting him.

"Oh. Um, normal," Blane admitted. "Not much is happening. Sheila's doing really well though, she's moving to Philadelphia next week."

"Aw, so soon! I bet the visitors will miss that."

"Yeah. And your day?"

"Just hanging out with Oscar," Falcon told him, drawing both of their gazes back to the others for a moment. "He doesn't make it into town often." Then, Falcon's gaze dropped to Roman's hand on Oscar's arm. He cleared his throat. "Pizza's here."

Blane had the sense Falcon was as interested in keeping them apart as he was, but he wasn't sure why.

Conversation flowed easily between them all over pizza, but every time Oscar started flirting with Roman, Blane would find some excuse to intervene before his friend could fall head over heels for yet another guy who would leave him —physically, this time, not just emotionally. Or, if it was the other way around and Roman was getting closer to Oscar, Falcon would interrupt.

Oddly, something itched the wrong way at Blane when that happened. When it happened again—Falcon brought up an art show when Roman was trying to talk about a museum he'd been to near Los Angeles—Blane finally cut Falcon off.

"Can I have a word?" At the curious gazes from the other two, Blane added weakly, "Wedding stuff."

Falcon cast him an odd look, too, but rose from his chair. "Yeah, of course. Back in a sec."

They strolled outside for a hint of cool, fresh air—as cool

as it got around here until December, anyway. Evening had fallen, which helped.

"What's up?" Falcon asked, his voice tight.

Blane sank onto the bench out front, ignoring the smokers on the other side of the doorway. "You were getting a little, um… tense there."

"So were you."

"Yeah." Blane could admit it, but he wasn't sure Falcon would like why. "I just think… they both travel a lot."

"Yeah. It'd be weird to have our friends hook up and then hurt each other."

Blane's eyebrows rose. Roman might sleep around, but he didn't deliberately hurt people's feelings or lead them on. If anything, he scared them off. "What do you mean?"

"Well, I think you're getting a little protective of Roman, aren't you? I guess… I'm that way with Oscar. He's my best friend, you know?"

Blane softened and smiled at Falcon, reaching out to touch his knee. "Yeah. I get it. I don't want Roman hurt, you don't want Oscar hurt."

"When you put it that way," Falcon murmured, his shoulders sinking as he drew a breath. "Yeah."

"But it's none of our decision anyway." Blane glanced around, then took Falcon's hand, and to his relief, Falcon let him. "I like that you're protective of him."

"I think it's natural. He's been hurt before."

"Yeah," Blane murmured immediately, nodding. "So has Roman. I know he looks tough, but he's got a soft heart."

Falcon smiled at him, his dimples showing up at last. "Doesn't sound like anyone I know."

"Oh, shut up," Blane grumbled as Falcon laughed. "Anyway, I guess… we have to trust them. They're adults. If they hook up and make it awkward, we'll deal with it later. It's not like that kind of stuff doesn't happen."

"Does it with your friends?" Falcon asked.

Blane had to think for a second. "Weirdly, no. *We* haven't hooked up, even if there's probably zero degrees of separation in our love lives. I don't think we ever made an outright pact not to, it just… I don't know."

"So you and Roman…"

"No!" Blane exclaimed, then laughed. "I mean, not that he's a bad guy, just—"

"No, no." Falcon chuckled. "It's like your brothers. Like me and Oscar. Just weird."

"Exactly." The tension between them had almost disappeared now. Then, Blane leaned in. "Why? Were you jealous?"

Falcon looked bashful for a moment, then looked away and cleared his throat. "So, uh. The wedding?"

Blane chewed his lip. Falcon was sending him all the right signals, but whenever he called him out on it, he changed the subject. It made it hard to focus on his thoughts. "Right. Did you want me to pick you up that morning? I'll come early with you, I know you agreed to do setup."

"Would you mind? You really don't have to. You're already doing me a huge favor," Falcon told him.

Blane shook his head and smiled. "Nah, I'm having fun fucking with the head of a guy who hurt a guy I like a lot."

Falcon's brows drew together for a moment like he was trying to figure that out, and then he looked embarrassed. "Oh! Right. Uh, cool."

Blane laughed under his breath and leaned in to kiss Falcon. Just briefly—it *was* the South, after all, but people didn't usually fuck with guys his size. "You're adorable. Let's get back in before they start playing footsie."

"Ew. Let's," Falcon agreed. "I'll text you the rest of the details, huh? Make sure we get coordinating outfits…"

"Perfect." Blane rose to his feet, and Falcon took his hand as they walked back in on Oscar and Roman laughing together about something.

I like Oscar. I just don't want him hurting my brother, and I guess vice versa. When Blane thought about it, he found it sweetly endearing that Falcon had that side to him.

And, apparently, a jealous side.

Whatever he says—or doesn't say—I think he feels the same way about me. Unlike Roman, trying his best to match up with everyone he met, Blane hadn't felt this certain about anyone in a long time. But taking it at this pace was killing him.

Blane couldn't wait for the weekend and the excuse to show Falcon what he'd get as his boyfriend, if all went well. But, on the other hand, thinking about it made the pressure ten times worse.

One day at a time.

CHAPTER

Nineteen

FALCON

Only sheer force of will kept Falcon from chewing off both thumbnails by Saturday morning. Oscar had stayed the night of their accidental double date, then left.

Leaving Falcon freaking the fuck out about the wedding.

Even though it was a tiny family affair and he and Blane had planned every detail of their backstory and nothing could possibly go wrong.

Right? Right.

He nearly jumped out of his skin at the knock on his door.

The anxiety he'd been stewing in for the past several days flowed away as soon as he saw Blane filling his doorframe and giving him that rare big smile.

And he looked gorgeous—tailored suit and tie. The color was coordinated (by Falcon's insistent text messages) to match Falcon's light pink shirt. He also looked like he belonged in this suit, unlike how he usually seemed to get itchy as soon as he wore so much as a button-down shirt.

It occurred to Falcon that maybe he was trying to impress his family.

"Oh, God." Falcon breathed out and reached out to hug Blane, leaning into his solid weight for a minute and pressing his forehead into his neck.

"Whoa. You look like you're the one getting married today," Blane teased, but he was gently rubbing Falcon's back. "Nervous for your sister? Or are you the best man?"

"Oh, I like my new sister-in-law. And no, they're not even having that kind of ceremony," Falcon admitted and pulled back. "I'm just nervous about how all this will go. You meeting my family and stuff. And Spencer," he quickly added as the pretense of their appearance together suddenly came back to him.

Blane winked. "Right. That doesn't make me feel nervous at all. I'll try to impress everyone."

"Oh, shit. No." Falcon blushed hard now. "No, I know you will. Just..."

"You're also coming out." Blane tapped his shoulder to move him aside, then gingerly picked up the meticulously wrapped artwork.

Falcon watched carefully to be sure Blane knew how to handle it, then snorted. Like *anyone* didn't know about him. "I guess."

"Come on. Let's get you there to set up. That should help the nerves," Blane told him.

Falcon relaxed at his tone of voice—confident and supportive, like he knew exactly the right prescription to help. "Thank you," he murmured.

Blane cast him an affectionate look, but he couldn't do much with the wrapped, framed artwork in his arms. "Do I get a hello kiss before I try to tackle these stairs with this, my boyfriend-for-today?"

And there it is. Falcon's heart jumped and his stomach churned at once. Hell, his toes curled into his stupid stiff formal shoes. "I—yeah," he croaked and leaned in to brush their lips together.

Warm but not exactly intimate, especially since he had to lean in around the corner of the painting.

"Well. I'll get more passion out of you after the champagne starts," Blane promised and winked.

The art easily fit into the trunk of Blane's car, and then they were off toward the venue, Falcon twisting his hands together in his lap.

"Hey." Blane took his hand and squeezed. "You look handsome today."

"So do you. Didn't I say that? You really do," Falcon smiled, lacing their fingers. "Delectable."

"Ohhh," Blane grinned. "Such a big word for me. Really?"

"The word is proportionate to the delectability of… well, all of you as well as parts," Falcon winked.

Blane laughed richly. "Why, thank you. Did you want to go over the backstory?"

Blane's attention to detail was adorable. Falcon nodded. "Just what happened in real life.

"But without so much fucking."

Falcon was startled into a laugh. It was odd for it to be this way around—Blane cheering up Falcon, not Falcon bugging him out of his shell. But it felt nice to be taken care of.

"And we've been together…?" Falcon prompted.

"It feels like forever," Blane finished immediately. "Then I do something adorably sappy." They'd decided it was best to dance around the question rather than outright lie.

Falcon's lips quirked into a smile. *I think we are, whether or not we're admitting it. And it does feel like forever already.*

"Okay, next right," Falcon directed as they pulled off the highway to the small winery his sister had chosen to host the wedding and, more importantly, reception—which just meant party.

The parking lot was nearly empty. Probably just Mom, Rosalina, and Jenny, plus a couple of their friends and the event staff.

"Not many people yet," Falcon told Blane with a bright smile that was much more confident than he felt.

"Leave the gift in the car?"

"They should have the tables set up already. But you can bring it in later."

"Can I?" Blane teased.

"What's the point of bringing my big burly boyfriend if he won't carry my things?" Falcon shook his head.

"Tsch. That lazy bastard trying to get out of work," Blane shook his head solemnly and leaned toward Falcon as he unbuckled.

Falcon kissed him for a few moments longer this time, relaxing. The feeling of Blane's cheek under his palm, the scent of him, his very presence filling up the car, made him feel safe. Warm.

"Ready?" Blane asked.

Falcon nodded once. No matter what was going to happen, there was no looking back now.

Hand in hand, they approached the entrance of the canopy set up next to one of the winery buildings.

"Falcon!" Rosalina had an armful of flowers that she

nearly dropped at the sight of him—and, presumably, Blane. "Oh my God. Mom! Falcon's here!"

Jenny appeared, too, and a couple of their friends that Falcon had met before occasionally.

Rosalina looked like she was about to burst, grinning ear to ear. One of her friends, Anna, took the flowers from her.

"Hey," Falcon greeted them all. He was acutely aware of all the eyes on them, his cheeks hot. "This is Blane."

"Blane Winters. I'm with him," Blane supplied with an amused lilt in his voice, since Falcon's voice had failed before he could do it. "I've been told I don't need an official invite. I hope he was right." Falcon squeezed his hand in thanks and got a squeeze in return. "Great to meet you all."

"Hi, Blane. I'm Julia," his mom said, brushing past his outstretched hand to hug him tightly and kiss his cheek, even though she had to stretch onto tiptoe to do it. "Welcome to our crazy Harper family!"

Rosalina and Jenny did the same and he hugged them back carefully, complimenting Rosalina's hair.

"Oh, the wedding styling isn't even done yet! I told them not to touch me before noon. Too much to set up before then!"

"And *I* said it's their wedding day and they should be relaxing," his mom clicked her tongue. "But they won't listen."

"I wonder where she gets the control freak tendencies from?" Falcon grinned at her, earning him a light clip on the ear.

"Don't mind my son," Mom said to Blane. "He gets *such* a thrill out of acting out."

Falcon laughed at how true it was.

"Oh, I won't. But if it's all the same, I think I'll be on my best behavior, ma'am," Blane saluted, and they all laughed.

That was it, then—as uneventful as could be, exactly how they knew he wanted it. Falcon's anxiety didn't vanish, but he certainly had one less worry.

His energy renewed, Falcon shooed Rosalina and Jenny off to prepare for their part in the day. "We've got this covered," he told them firmly.

Falcon couldn't stop smiling as he threw himself into setting up tables inside and rows of chairs in front of the veiled and vine-covered arbor. He set out flower arrangements while Blane climbed ladders to string up lights inside the tent.

He might have been guarded at work, but Blane chatted freely with his mom and his sister's friends as they worked, and Falcon loved listening in.

They stopped for a quick lunch break as the catering and event staff arrived to take over the final preparations. Falcon found himself laughing along with the stories Blane was telling about animals misbehaving on the veterinary table.

But his mom wasn't going to let time slip by, or any of them slack off.

"The guests will be arriving any minute now."

And that meant another round of introductions—to aunts, grandparents, and family friends—but this time, Falcon had no fear.

How could he, when Blane's hand fit perfectly in his own, and the day was sunny, and everything... *everything...* seemed perfect?

CHAPTER
Twenty
BLANE

As weddings went, Blane was impressed at how smoothly organized everything seemed to be.

Granted, he didn't have to slip off and supervise the brides like Falcon's mom did, and the event staff were taking care of all the remaining setup, but there weren't any zip-tie or duct tape emergencies that he could see.

"Time to meet the rest of the family." Falcon leaned into him as they lingered around the rows of empty chairs outside. At least, judging by the seating, there were only going to be fifty guests or less. Not many at all.

Blane wrapped his arm around Falcon's shoulders and nodded, watching as Rosalina's friends greeted guests and directed them through to the vineyard setup. "Less nervous?"

"Way," Falcon agreed with a smile. "Thanks for… all the help. You really didn't have to."

"What else are boyfriends for?" Blane smiled. He was enjoying milking it, especially since Falcon got flustered every time he mentioned their pretense.

"About that…"

But before he could speak, a gasp from behind them. "Falcon! You were telling the truth!"

Blane watched Falcon's face close off in a way he'd never seen before, and he instantly hated whoever it was.

They turned to see, and Falcon nodded once at the lanky, well-dressed man leaning against the nearest chair. "Spencer."

Now I really *hate him.*

"This is Blane," Falcon continued. "Blane, Spencer."

"Pleasure," Spencer said in a tone that made it clear it wasn't.

Blane matched it. "Likewise." He inclined his head and watched as Spencer reached out to try for a hug and Falcon didn't move. If he tried to force the issue, Blane was prepared to intervene.

But, perhaps sensing this, Spencer didn't. Instead, he stretched and shoved his hands back in his pockets. "Sooo. You two, huh?"

"Us two," Falcon agreed.

"How long?"

"Feels like forever now," Blane said, sliding his arm around Falcon's shoulders and smiling thinly at Spencer. His patience for assholes—that didn't belong to people he liked—was limited, and Spencer was treading way over the line.

Blane remembered his role: keep Falcon calm and away from Spencer. It didn't stop him wanting to chuck Spencer into the vineyard, except that it would be a waste of grapes.

Spencer's expression was barely a smile. "Huh. I bet it hasn't been."

"How about you?" Falcon asked. "Found yourself a nice girl to introduce to your family yet?"

There was a distinctly bitter edge to his voice that Blane

hadn't heard before, too. Blane wasn't sure he liked this side of the normally annoyingly optimistic and cheerful Falcon at all.

"Nah. There are other things in life," Spencer responded with a strangely casual smile. "But good for you, going after what you want."

Blane nodded courteously. "I think I see more relatives to meet. Falcon?"

"See you," Falcon half-waved at Spencer and turned as Blane steered him toward the entrance of the tent.

As they walked, Blane murmured, "You all right?"

"Yeah. Better than I expected." Falcon seemed to come to when Blane looked at him, stirring out of his reverie. "It's just weird, seeing him."

Blane fought back the tinge of jealousy. *He said he was over him. You should trust that.* "Right. As loathe as I am to meet the relatives…"

"Oh, Aunt Vera will love you."

"What is *with* your family's names?" Blane laughed quietly.

Falcon grinned. "I don't know. It's just a tradition. We always say we like to be… distinctive."

"You certainly are," Blane murmured, squeezing Falcon around the shoulders.

Falcon turned an adorable shade of red and grabbed the closest family member for introductions—as it turned out, Vera.

"Finally!" Vera exclaimed when Blane took her hand. She shook it free and hugged him instead, kissing him on the cheek. "I've heard Falcon got the stick out of his ass at last. Or maybe *in*. It's marvelous to meet the man who made him *finally* crack his code of silence."

Falcon went red and stuttered while Blane tried not to laugh.

"Er… good to meet you, too," Blane managed.

"Oh, pah. You can't tell me we didn't know you were *seeing* men," Vera told Falcon matter-of-factly, patting his cheek. "But your sister beat you to the punch on getting the balls to tell us. I don't know if I have any rainbow pins left for *your* wedding."

Falcon half-raised his hand as if stunned, turning his gaze to Blane for help.

Blane covered his mouth and cleared his throat. "Um. It's great to meet the family, too."

Vera was undaunted. "There was you and that boy—Spencer. Is he here today?"

Falcon's flushed cheeks faded to pale and his eyes widened. "Don't—why do you—did you know?"

"He *is* here," Blane added in a murmur, although nobody was in earshot.

Vera scowled. "Did he break your heart? I always suspected. I'll bend his ear."

"No…" Falcon trailed off, but he fidgeted. "Look, you can't tell anyone."

This will last all of ten seconds. Blane bit his tongue and glanced sideways at Falcon, but he didn't seem to notice.

"He didn't want to tell anyone about us. When I finally told him it was my way or the highway, he ran the other way."

"Not even your side of the family? Coward." Vera snorted. "Oh, I'll *definitely* bend his ear."

"Aunt Vera—"

But she was off to the refreshments table, still shaking her head.

Blane chuckled as Falcon swivelled his head to look at him. "What did you expect? Does she normally keep family gossip to herself?" he asked. "She seems rather... ah... open."

Falcon winced. "Good point."

"I have the feeling this is all going to go..." Falcon trailed off.

Blane put a finger over Falcon's lips. "Not on your sister's big day."

"Quick, find me some wood to knock on."

Figuring better than to say it out loud, Blane just gave Falcon a dirty grin and a wink.

Falcon broke out laughing. "Yeah, I walked into that one."

"Like I walked into you." Blane wrapped his arm around Falcon's waist and led him to the opposite side of the aisle from Spencer, near the front.

Knocking on the wooden chair did absolutely nothing, but it seemed to make Falcon feel better when Blane caught his eye and did it.

Falcon smiled at him, leaning into his side as the rest of the small wedding party began finding their seats.

Everyone will get through today perfectly fine.

It turned out to be the best wedding ceremony Blane had ever been to. Mainly because it was the shortest, but it was also sweet—no being handed off by anyone, just both brides entering, hand-in-hand.

Flower petals were thrown, the guests were encouraged to holler and cheer when they kissed over their new rings and a bunch of flowers. The vows were short and lacked any weird connotations of either of them suddenly being the property of the other.

Everything about it was a coming-together and a beginning, not an end. It was the kind of wedding Blane wanted.

Someday.

Not immediately. Not necessarily with the man next to him. But if things worked out that way…

Blane didn't even realize he was looking at Falcon and not ahead until he reeled backward, greenery and blossoms nearly flattening his face. Falcon's hand was suddenly there, too.

"I think it was supposed to be yours," Falcon grinned as he held the bouquet in front of Blane's face. "I hope you weren't angling for a nose job."

Blane barely resisted the response he wanted to give, but he saw the corners of Falcon's eyes crinkle, like he was reading his mind. "Thanks for saving my face. Literally, too."

Falcon was offering him the bouquet, and suddenly it was his turn to be embarrassed and very conscious of those around him cheering and laughing.

Is this… does this… no, play along. Don't take him for granted. Blane gulped but took the bouquet, then leaned in to kiss Falcon.

Rosalina's cheer was the loudest of all, and she had a wickedly purposeful glint in her eye.

She totally intended that. Blane shot her a half-glare, half-thankful look, not even sure himself which emotion was stronger.

Her shameless grin back at him said it all, and Blane was surprised at the emotion that took hold within his chest: warm, happy, safe.

Belonging.

They were welcoming him with open arms, and he was deceiving them. Maybe less than he fooled himself into thinking, but he had to fix this.

Jenny's bouquet had gone to the other side of the aisle, where an older man in perhaps his seventies was kissing someone Blane assumed was his wife. Those around them *awwed* at the sight. Even Blane was unashamed of how warm and fuzzy it made him feel.

"That's enough of this romance crap," Rosalina called out, to surprised laughter. "You're here to party. Let's party!"

Blane thought that an excellent idea indeed, and before Falcon could see his face, he stood up and stretched, the bouquet in one hand. "Drinks?"

Falcon looped his arm through Blane's, his voice soft. "Drinks."

CHAPTER
Twenty-One
FALCON

BLANE'S PHONE HAD NEVER RUNG WHEN THEY WERE ON A DATE before.

Maybe it was all the champagne talking—Blane wasn't partaking, but he obediently fetched Falcon new glasses at regular intervals—but Falcon didn't like it one little bit.

"Sorry, hon. I gotta get this."

"Fine, fine," Falcon murmured. While Blane answered, he found a chair against the edge of the tent to sit in and rest his feet. God only knew what hour it was now, but the dancing and partying and toasting had made the day fly by. It must be late at night now.

When Blane came back, he was wobbly—no, that was Falcon's vision. Falcon cleared his throat and sat straight, hoping he wasn't weaving.

"Babe, I'm sorry." Blane crouched in front of him and took his hands. His hands were warm and strong. Falcon liked his hands. "The zoo called."

"The… zoo? But it's Saturday."

Blane squeezed lightly and gave him a frown of apology.

"I know. Sorry. It's an emergency call-out. Or call-in, I suppose."

Well, Falcon couldn't be angry about that. He was a little melancholy—after such an amazing day by Blane's side, the night would lose some of its sparkle without him around.

And this could be it for us. After all that time planning, this day just flies by, and then he's gone.

But an emergency was an emergency. It wasn't like this happened every day. "Go save animals, and stuff," he murmured, leaning in for a kiss.

"I will. Text me later, huh? Tell me you got home safe," Blane told him. "You're taking a taxi, right?"

Falcon nodded. "Yes, sir."

"Good." Blane smiled, then rose to his feet. "See you."

"See you around." Falcon rolled his head back against the canvas tent wall and closed his eyes for a moment.

When Falcon opened his eyes again, it must have been more than a second later, because there was a warm presence at his side, a head on his shoulder. He smiled for a few moments, until the familiar woodsy scent hit like a gut punch.

He pulled back so fast Spencer nearly slipped off the chair into his lap. "Hey," Spencer protested, swaying.

Why was Spencer holding his phone?

"You dropped this," Spencer told him, handing it over. "Drunkard."

"I'm not drunk," Falcon snorted. His head was a little clearer with Spencer next to him, but not in a good way. In the way that meant he wanted to throttle the twerp who was smirking at him like he'd snuck in a cuddle.

He felt dirty.

"*Spencer.*"

Both of them nearly jumped out of their seats as Aunt Vera's voice crashed across the dance floor, preceding her. She was standing there a moment later, staring down her nose at him, arms folded.

Oh, shit. She's going for it. Falcon's eyes widened and his lips pressed together.

"Huh?"

"Don't *huh* me, young man." She tapped her foot, and everyone nearby went quiet. Vera might not have been the oldest woman in the family, but she was the matriarch.

What Aunt Vera said went, and even Spencer knew that. He gulped and rose to his feet, folding his hands behind his back.

"You broke my nephew's heart." Falcon stuttered, but Aunt Vera held up a hand and he went obediently silent. "And yes, he'll say you didn't, but we all saw it. It's taken him this long to let a nice, sweet man sweep him off his feet after you. You should be ashamed of yourself. If Rosalina had any idea…" Vera snorted and waved her hand dismissively, as if he weren't worthy of another second of attention. "Skulk out of here and don't darken this family's doorstep again."

Spencer reeled, looking more and more offended by the second. "Whatever this lying asshole told you, it's not true. We were never serious."

"*What?*" Falcon exclaimed, his gut clenching. That was pretty fucking far from the truth.

"I don't need details," Vera said, still airily dismissive. "Trying to sneak up for a cuddle when his boyfriend's away? Bless your heart for thinking that would fly around here. I've called a taxi. Shoo and fuck yourself sideways with a cactus." She flicked her fingers again.

The mix of exceeding politeness and vulgarity made Falcon burst out laughing.

Spencer snarled something under his breath and spun on his heel to wobble out of the tent.

"Aunt Vera… We weren't… I mean, you didn't have to."

"Shhh. I didn't like the shape of his nose. It was that or reshape it."

Falcon laughed much too hard at that for a minute before he rose to his feet and pulled her in for a tight hug. "Thank you."

Just like when he'd been growing up, she was safe and warm and present, rubbing his back gently. "Don't let assholes ruin your day."

"It's not *mine*," he pointed out.

She let go and winked. "Isn't it? Now, I have some dancing to do. Everyone out of the way!"

Falcon stared after her, mouth opening and closing. He wasn't quite sure what he meant, but he had a sneaking suspicion…

She's always been way too perceptive.

Maybe it could be his day. Maybe that ache in his chest that started the moment Blane left, that he couldn't deal with when he was a little drunk, meant something more. Maybe all of this was a sign.

His phone went off, and the text on the screen confused him. It was from Blane.

Are you sober enough? Safe? Happy?

Followed by another.

I can't. You must know why by now. Please don't break my heart.

Then his eye was caught by the edge of the message before in the conversation—a photo. He scrolled up.

It was a photo of him with his head rolled back against the canvas. With the wrinkles, it looked kind of like sheets under his head. And Spencer's head was on his shoulder, his lips close to Falcon's neck.

A full-body shudder coursed through him, and that was before he saw the caption.

Things changed. I thought you should know first. Join us after work?

"Oh, shit," Falcon breathed out. "That... cocksucking douchecanoe asswipe!"

He was going to *strangle* Spencer with his *own bare hands.* Or he would, if he could stand straight. But the blood was rushing to his head, and he couldn't feel his hands, and his chest was tight with panic.

When he made his way to the tent entrance, there was no sign of Spencer in the lot. There was a taxi, though, so he made a beeline to claim it. He couldn't stay at the party in this mood.

Once he was in the back seat, he pulled his phone out to stare at the photo and messages again. Every time he reread them, he felt dirty, from head to toe. How had Spencer even remembered his phone passcode, this many years later? For fuck's sake, why hadn't he changed it?

Was jealousy enough to make Spencer try to break up the relationship? Did he think that breaking up with Blane would make Falcon come crawling back to him?

When his phone screen darkened, then went to sleep, he could still see the image burned into his brain: Spencer's head right there, where Blane's belonged. The filthy, slimy git's hands on his phone. Thank God they hadn't been alone, or they might have gone elsewhere, too.

He wouldn't... would he? Falcon felt sick. He suddenly

doubted himself. If Spencer was the kind of man who'd do this, where would he have stopped? All these questions swirled around Falcon's head, but the biggest one of all was the one he was afraid to even directly think.

Falcon felt sick. He needed a shower. He needed caffeine, no matter if it was midnight or not.

Maybe that would make him feel calm enough to come up with a response and an explanation. It was going to be so lame—*that wasn't me, he stole my phone, it's not what it looks like.*

Blane had to believe him. He had to. There wasn't exactly a sex tape or anything, just one carefully-framed photo and message. Blane knew how he felt. Blane knew he hated Spencer.

Tonight was supposed to be my night, and maybe I fucked it all up.

A life without Blane was not a life he ever wanted to imagine. If tears trickled down the crease of his nose in the darkness of the taxi backseat, nobody had to know.

"Actually," Falcon cleared his throat, leaning forward. "Sir? I want to go to a different address."

CHAPTER

Twenty~Two

BLANE

EMERGENCY C-SECTIONS WERE NEVER FUN. THEY WERE EVEN less fun with complications, late at night, after an exhausting evening of dancing, with just one vet tech to assist him and a worried keeper hovering around like *he* was giving birth himself.

But the mother and baby lived, and that was all that mattered. New life in the world. New beginnings. It made Blane smile.

His eyes were heavy, his hands still shaky with the adrenaline he'd carefully compartmentalized to display a calm and in-control attitude for the benefit of everyone round. He barely remembered stumbling to the back for his phone and car keys.

But he sure as hell remembered his screen lighting up with a photo of the guy he'd been seconds away from asking out, and that guy's douchebag ex-boyfriend.

Getting way, way too close.

He wanted to drop his phone, or better yet, fling it—hurl it back into the locker, whether or not it cracked.

It's not like him. But then, you barely know him. Why the fuck did you let yourself fall in love first?

Blane knew it was unreasonable to expect himself *not* to feel what he had since the moment they met, but he didn't care. It was way too late and he was way too tired to be logical about it.

Hell, for a dark minute, he wished Spencer had been on his operating table.

But what if Spencer makes him happy?

He made himself wait until he was in his car to answer. The parking lot was silent and empty, and nobody could hear his breath tighten and choke in his throat.

His first concern was sobriety and safety. If Spencer had gotten him drunk, or God forbid, drugged him... he would hunt that man to the end of the earth. But the awful possibility that Falcon was just drunk enough to do what he really wanted... it wouldn't leave Blane's head.

So he composed a message, his hands shaking, trying not to let on how badly it hurt.

Are you sober enough? Safe? Happy?

As much as his heart was breaking, and as much as this had come like a bolt out of the blue, these things happened. Chemistry reignited. Sparks flew. It was normal. Normal. It happened all the time.

His thoughts were erratic now, his hand clenching so tightly his nails bit into his palm like tiny scalpels.

Fuck normal. *Fuck* anyone who tried to tell him Falcon didn't love him. He'd seen the look on Falcon's face when he saw Spencer. There was no love there, even deep inside. There wasn't even enough hatred to turn into one wild night of no-holds-barred passion.

But what if he'd missed the signs? What if the offer was real?

He had to treat it like the truth until he found out otherwise. The evidence stacked up: it sounded like Falcon's typing. It was sure as hell a picture of Falcon, and it was from Falcon's number. Falcon had a lock on his phone—who didn't these days? And Falcon had been drinking. Alcohol made people do stupid things.

So Blane carefully typed out one more text, back-spacing when his blurry vision made him hit the wrong letter.

I can't. You must know why by now. Please don't break my heart.

He couldn't bring himself to believe it was real, but it also made sense in a fucked-up kind of way.

Nothing ever worked out for him. He should have known better than to fall for a guy so fast, trust him so much. After all, the whole goddamn wedding was supposedly a sham.

But it didn't feel like one until now, he argued with himself.

Blane slammed the steering wheel with his fists, and as quickly as that, the anger bled out of him. He rested his forehead on the wheel until he could think straight enough to drive. All he had to worry about at first was getting home.

Tomorrow morning would come. And so would the truth. And, if he had to, Blane would walk away and wait for a better man.

But his heart told him the truth: Falcon was it. Falcon was the one he wanted. Falcon was the one right now pressed against some slimeball who wanted a pretty trophy boy, who didn't see his sweet heart and his clever brain and his compassion and insight and…

Don't. Blane choked back the thoughts and focused on driving. *Start the car. Shoulder checks. Buckle up.*

Routine took over.

Routine took him home through suburbia.

Routine kept him from running any red lights, late as it was.

But routine didn't tell him what to do when he pulled up in his driveway and found a man sitting on his porch, head in his hands.

Every thought Blane had tucked away came roaring back until his hands shook as he climbed out of the car. "Falcon?"

"It wasn't me." The man's voice cracked, and Blane strode for him to comfort him before he even thought twice about it. Falcon couldn't meet his eyes, but his hands were wringing one another.

Blane took him by the shoulder and pulled him to his feet, his voice low and urgent. He didn't care that they were on his front porch, within earshot of the neighbors. The night pressed around them, claustrophobic even in the open air. "Did he hurt you? Falcon. *Please* tell me. It's not your fault." *If he did...*

Falcon jerkily shook his head. "I fell asleep for a minute. I woke up with his head... with that photo. At the tent. At the wedding!" He held fistfuls of Blane's shirt, but he was upright now, stone-cold sober and desperate. "I never left with him, he stole my phone and texted, please believe me."

Of course he did. Blane blinked a few times, then pulled Falcon in to hug him tightly. "Of course... of course I do!"

"You... do?" Falcon's voice was faint.

Blane pulled back and studied his face, then took him silently by the arm to lead him into the house. "Come in. You look like you're in shock."

Falcon laughed under his breath. "You're going all hot zoo vet on me, aren't you?"

"I can't help it." The relief that overwhelmed Blane made him laugh, even if the sound was strange to his own ears. "I'm just… just glad."

Falcon sank onto the sofa next to him, and leaned into his chest immediately, pressing his face into Blane's neck. Like Spencer had held him.

Blane's lip curled. "So, you fell asleep, he took a photo, and texted me a bunch of lies? To try to get between us?"

Falcon's voice choked. "Yes. Shit. God. When you put it that way… I'm so stupid. I should have texted, or anything… but I didn't think you'd believe me if it's not face-to-face…"

More than anything else, Blane's mental alarm bells were going off now, but he stayed calm and kept his arms lightly around Falcon's shoulders. "Because he wouldn't have believed you, back when you dated?"

Falcon went still for a minute, and then the tension seemed to bleed out of him. "You're right. Shit. He'd get jealous of my high school friends, even though he didn't want to be *with* me… He wanted the best of all worlds." He drew a breath and let it out. "It brought all that back. I thought I didn't care about him or any of that."

Blane kissed the top of his head. "Once someone's mistreated an animal in my care, it takes a long time to build up trust again. I have animals who will sit up and stay still when I vaccinate them, and I have animals who are terrified of me looking at them."

Falcon chuckled. "You have any falcons who panic and flap around like idiots?"

"No. But I have falcons who react completely appropriately given the way people have treated them," Blane murmured and hugged him tighter. "It would have all come out in the morning, but... I'm so glad you came to me tonight."

"Mmm."

Falcon was so much braver than he knew, and that was just the cherry on top of the ice cream sundae. Blane wanted it all. "Hon? I liked tonight. Let's forget about this last hour of bullshit, huh?"

Falcon nodded immediately, his hands resting on Blane's arm and thigh now as he relaxed in Blane's hold. "Yeah. Yeah, tonight was perfect."

"Almost perfect," Blane murmured.

Falcon was looking at him now, that desperate yet fearful look gone. Blane no longer wanted to put Spencer through a wall. Or at least, *he* could wait until tomorrow to do that. "Why?"

"I want us to be a real thing."

Falcon was smiling now, but trying to hide it. "You mean...?"

"Yeah, I mean," Blane echoed, scratching his back lightly. "If you want me."

"Of *course* I want you, you idiot," Falcon exclaimed, straightening up indignantly. "Why else would I be here?"

Blane laughed loudly. "Oh, *I'm* not allowed a moment of insecurity?"

That made Falcon grin back at him. "You wouldn't let me get away with it."

"I won't let you get away with anything," Blane murmured with a wink. "Not my gorgeous boyfriend."

Falcon flushed and grinned and squirmed against him, all at the same time, and it was probably the cutest thing Blane had ever seen him do.

"You looked *hot* tonight, by the way," Blane added,

walking his fingers down Falcon's chest. "In your suit and tie."

"Matching you."

"Matching me. No wonder that asshole was jealous." Blane stopped to hook his finger through Falcon's belt. "We're too good together."

"Too good to be true?" Falcon murmured.

It hit Blane in the heart, but he stopped, then shook his head. "I thought that, until now. Or I would have asked you weeks ago."

"Doesn't matter. We're here now, together, and that asshole just… well. He just did the opposite of what he wanted." Falcon smiled at him, mischievous and smug. "So, take me to bed."

Blane growled playfully as he swept Falcon into his arms. "Oh, I will."

He didn't want an ounce of the pain they'd just been through to bother them in the morning. Wedding nights were for lovers, and they were going to make it a hell of a memorable one for all the right reasons.

The exhaustion was almost forgotten with the excitement rushing through him now. This was a much more productive outlet for his adrenaline than sitting in his car worrying about a future alone and untrusting.

He hardly wanted to let Falcon go, but he had to set the man on the bed so they could start tearing the clothes off each other's bodies.

Blane hadn't bothered putting his tie back on after work, but Falcon wasn't taking his time with the buttons on his shirt. He, meanwhile, had more clothes to deal with, because Falcon was still immaculately dressed from the wedding.

"Motherfucking layers," Blane groused when he finally

had his boyfriend shirtless under him.

Falcon chuckled. "That's what makes suits hot, and you know it."

"And now I have to deal with these pants?" Blane gestured. "Ridiculous."

"I know," Falcon grinned. "Pants should be illegal. Then I could see your hot ass a lot more."

"We can make them illegal in our household."

Falcon raised his brow. "Our household?"

Oh, that does sound a little... Blane cleared his throat. "You know. A house. When we're both in it. And, eventually, when we live together?"

"Good answer." Falcon leaned up to kiss him. "I want that. Now keep taking my pants off before I jizz in them."

Blane grinned. He slid his hands along Falcon's arms until their fingers laced, pressing his hands to the bed as he leaned down to kiss Falcon hard.

Their tongues slid wildly along each other, lips claiming and clashing rather than gently sliding. Sweet and slow could come later. They needed it hard, dirty, and *now*.

Blane kissed Falcon's throat, and slowly worked down the center of his body toward his belt, making his lover squirm by focusing on his nipples for as long as he could stand it.

When he finally let go of Falcon's hands, face at crotch-level, his hands slid to Falcon's groin. He cupped the hardness through thin fabric, rubbing with the heel of his hand until Falcon writhed.

"Don't you fucking tease me," Falcon growled.

The animalistic need awoke the same in Blane, who growled right back, "I won't waste a minute. I want you spread-eagled and moaning for every inch of my cock."

Blane could take away every bad thing for a few minutes,

make their whole world narrow to the two of them, and his head spun with how much he wanted to.

"Yes," Falcon panted, helping Blane shove the fabric down and pull it off his legs to leave him naked. "Oh, Jesus, yes. Fuck me, Blane. Show me who my boyfriend is."

Blane stripped himself as fast as he could, then shoved their clothes aside with a sweep of his arm and pushed Falcon's legs up over his shoulders.

"Oh my God, are—*yes!*" Falcon groaned when Blane interrupted him by running his tongue around that tight little hole.

Blane kissed and sucked around it, bending Falcon in two and pressing his knees to his chest. The better access he had, the more he could run his tongue along sensitive nerves, watching as Falcon squeezed in little involuntary twitches of pleasure.

And the noises Falcon made—loose and unrestrained whimpers, moans, grunts of pleasure—made Blane throb for him. He desperately wanted to be inside the wet, ready opening.

He let Falcon have a minute with his own two fingers inside himself, watching those delicate hands at work. Then, Blane playfully sucked on his pinky.

"You motherfucking… if *that's* not a tease," Falcon gasped.

"No. This is." Blane sucked the tip of Falcon's cock into his mouth, smirking as Falcon pushed into him and jolted, shuddering with need. Falcon's cock hit the back of his throat and he swallowed, sucking hard and mercilessly for a few seconds.

Then he pulled Falcon's hand out and away and pulled his own mouth off that velvety, hard shaft. He left Falcon wet and empty and whimpering for more, but not for long.

When Blane grabbed the condom, Falcon grabbed his hand. "You get tested?"

"Of course," Blane murmured. "You?"

"Mmhmm." Falcon grinned. "Such a responsible man. If it's just us, let's not."

Blane smiled at him and tossed the condom aside again. "It's just us." He pressed the tip of his dick against Falcon, and sank inside easily, past the rings of tight muscle. His hands returned to the backs of Falcon's knees to hold him down while he slid in, feeling the sensation build inch by inch.

"Yes yes yes," Falcon gasped, his own hands closing around his knees, nails biting into skin to leave little white marks.

Blane slid his hands away from Falcon's legs and instead cupped his cheek, then his cock. "Fucking gorgeous. All of you. Head to toe. I need you."

"You've got me," Falcon whispered, tightening around Blane, locking their bodies together for a few seconds before he relaxed. "Fuck me hard, baby. I need *you*."

Blane shifted his weight to his knees and braced himself on the headboard above Falcon, angling his hips so he could drive in as deep as possible with every single thrust.

The bed rattled under them, and he didn't care. *This* was the meaning of fucking—this raw, electric-edged current of pleasure that ran under his skin, igniting his brain and body at once with energy he hadn't even known he'd had left in him tonight.

With every thrust, he pushed deep into Falcon. The grunts and moans spilling through the air came from both of them now. Skin on skin, hot and sweating, it was hard to tell where they began and ended, especially when he pulled

Falcon's legs over his shoulders so Falcon's hands were free to tangle in the back of his hair.

"I love you," Falcon breathed out. "I fuckin' do. And I don't care who knows it."

Blane grinned and ran his hand down to Falcon's cock. "Is that the sex talking? Do you love me more now?"

"Mmm!" Falcon writhed for a few moments and panted for breath when Blane started stroking him, even with a limited range between their bodies. "No, but yes!"

"Good. Because I love you too," Blane whispered, letting go of the headboard to cup Falcon's cheek. "And I wanna make you come so hard you forget your own name."

Falcon's lips parted, his hazy eyes focusing on Blane's for a few moments. "W-Well... I'm almost... there," he whispered. Every stroke of Blane's hand, every pump of his cock into him, made Falcon clench around him and twitch, his body tightening.

"That's it, baby," Blane moaned, captivated by every expression across his face. Falcon was wracked with pleasure, and Blane wanted to see that look on his face every goddamn day.

Seeing every one of Falcon's reactions made him burn with need, his own body tight and throbbing. It was all he could do to hold back from the few more sharp, erratic thrusts he needed and keep them deep, rubbing against the spot inside Falcon and the length outside at the same time.

Until Falcon arched his back, his chest pushing up against Blane's as he gasped for breath. He might not remember his own name, but Blane's name poured out like a prayer and a curse word all in one. Wet warmth coated his stomach and Blane's hand, and he squeezed Blane's sensitive length inside him like he never wanted to let it go.

Blane let go of Falcon and grabbed the bed to fuck him hard and fast. And then he was there, blackness teasing the edges of his vision from his sheer focus on the tight, warm, *loving* body he was inside. A groan echoed from his chest as Falcon rubbed his neck and back. His legs still draped over Blane's shoulders as Blane's pace finally slowed.

"Oh, fuck," Blane managed after a few moments of catching his breath. He was still deep inside Falcon, his cock half-hard and softening as stickiness from passion and sweat coated them both. "You okay?"

"Never been better," Falcon whispered, his legs opening and sliding off Blane's shoulders so he lay spread-eagled on the bed.

Blane nestled between his thighs and let his weight rest on Falcon, cupping his cheeks. "You're… beautiful."

"Shut up and let me breathe," Falcon whispered, but his lips twitched into a smile.

Blane managed a laugh. "No. I'll tell you you're beautiful 'til the cows come home."

"I'm sure it's significantly earlier than this," Falcon mumbled. "You're the vet. You oughta know that."

Blane laughed, and suddenly he couldn't stop laughing. Falcon's melodic voice joined him, his arms wrapped around Blane, and they were laughing together about nothing important, but everything, too.

Exhausted, but together. That was all that mattered. Blane's hand took Falcon's, their fingers slid into the gaps between each other's, and Falcon didn't pull back.

Finally, Falcon was here, in his grasp—the bird who returned when Blane let him go.

Blane slept.

CHAPTER
Twenty~Three
FALCON

"You didn't have to put up with an ounce of that bullshit."

"Mom!" Falcon laughed, as much from surprise as relief. "No, I know. But I wanted to beat him on my own, you know?"

His sister's sigh was loud and audible from the tablet on the coffee table. She and Jenny were on their honeymoon now, but even distance didn't stop her joining the loving scolding the women of the family were currently giving Falcon.

"She's right," Rosalina told him. "I asked you if you wanted to uninvite him."

Aunt Vera shook her head, her tea cup between her palms. "I should have kicked him so hard his nuts would have gone on vacation."

Apparently the word had spread through the entire wedding party that Spencer was a no-good creep, and furthermore, that he was Falcon's ex. Falcon wasn't exactly unhappy about it, either.

"But I faced him, and… well, Aunt Vera scared him off. But I didn't want to just hide from him. I'm done hiding from anything. Or hiding anything, too."

"Including the cute little boy toy you've got yourself?" That was Jenny, leaning into the camera with a wicked grin.

Falcon flipped her off. "He's not a *boy toy*, he's… oh, shut up."

He's my boyfriend.

And soon he was gonna be meeting Blane's friends—significant brothers, he'd called them, which made Falcon laugh. He was nervous as hell about it but trying not to let on. Meeting a guy's friends meant… well, commitment. They were serious. All that stuff he'd been too afraid to even hope for.

"Manners, now," Mom scolded, but she didn't really mean it. She was smiling, too.

"He *is* dishy, isn't he?" Aunt Vera, his mother's sister, elbowed her. "Your son's got good taste."

"Both of my children do," Mom said, which made Falcon and Rosalina roll their eyes while Jenny beamed.

"Actually, guys… Spencer didn't just fail at getting between us, he pushed us a lot closer together." Falcon sheepishly smiled. "It started off as… well, we weren't really *boyfriends*."

"Always test-drive before you take it home for good," Vera nodded wisely.

Falcon laughed. "Aunt Vera!"

"She's right, though." Now he knew his mom was aiming to embarrass. "But you're official now?"

They didn't really need to know the whole story. Hell, they'd been halfway to official before the night even began—

it had just taken the twerp getting between them to drive them into saying anything. "Yeah. Yeah, that's right."

"Well, we're all happy for you!" Mom told him, then leaned in. "More tea?"

Falcon chuckled. "Yeah. Thanks, Mom."

"Oh! Falcon!" His sister clapped her hands. "I have a friend who loved your meerkat painting. Her boss is some super-rich dude, she's a PA and makes a ton of money, so she has to get him expensive gifts… and his wife loves meerkats."

"And?" Falcon prompted carefully, anticipation stirring.

"And she'll commission you to do a series. I'll give her your email, if you want—"

"Um, *yeah*, I want!" Falcon almost launched himself to his feet. Four commissions at once was a nice chunk of cash. "Thank you, sis. Jesus. That's amazing."

Vera patted his arm. "That means you'll have to hang around the zoo more often, doesn't it? Where that hunk of yours works…"

"I don't know how you'll manage it." Jenny nodded seriously.

Falcon laughed and waved them off. How right they were. "Oh, shut up, guys." But he didn't even want to joke that he shouldn't have told them.

Everything was too damn perfect as it was.

Twenty-Four

BLANE

"HEY, DO WE HAVE A FEW MINUTES AFTER LUNCH?"

Blane looked up from his sandwich at Gregory. "All the dailies are done." The routine yearly exams, vaccinations and deworming, prescription refills and food prep took up a good part of their mornings. Even in a small zoo where vets acted partly as keepers, there was always work to be done. "But I've got a lab report to do, and blood counts. Why?"

Gregory frowned. "Dianne told me all the vets and techs are being called in for a meeting after lunch."

All-department meetings were never good. A chill ran down Blane's spine as he assessed the possibilities. He'd just gotten permission to ask Falcon to help with the next animal painting session—surely if someone had a problem with that, it would be a one-on-one meeting. "Right. Well, I guess we'll find out. Do you know what's up?"

"No idea." Gregory sat opposite him, then nodded. "Do you mind company today?"

Blane opened his mouth to ask why he wouldn't, then almost cringed. He'd had enough days being surly in the lunch room. Gregory had always given him space, but this week, he'd felt a little less… well, under pressure.

"Yeah, of course. Go ahead. Sorry if I've ever… you know." Blane waved his sandwich. "Bitten your head off."

Gregory laughed under his breath as he eyed Blane. "Not around the animals. That's all that matters. But thanks. Where's this new, improved Blane coming from? His new boyfriend rubbing off on him?"

"Probably," Blane admitted with a laugh. "I didn't even yell at the woman pounding on the glass earlier. I just told her to imagine someone knocking on her bedroom window while she slept and she got all red and stopped."

"You didn't bite anyone's head off? Impressive. I'll believe it when I see it," Gregory told him.

"Well, she didn't understand what it does to the animals, I don't think. People are desperate for attention. Maybe to validate that the animals like them and find them interesting." Blane nodded philosophically. "Makes the zoo feel less weird, I suppose, if it's a mutual curiosity."

"Okaaay," Gregory answered, his lips quirking. "If you've been reading up on your Foucault on lunch hours, I might start giving them a miss."

Blane snorted. "Thanks." He was done lunch anyway, so he threw away his trash. "What time's the meeting?"

"In ten minutes."

"May as well walk over there early."

He fell into step beside his coworker, his mind already on the afternoon's chores. The morning tended to be filled with scheduled and routine work, and then helping keepers prepare lunch. In the afternoon came the fun stuff like animal enrichment—and the less-fun emergencies.

But every day was different. Falcon seemed to get that now, even if he'd looked at it as a nine-to-five job at first.

All his thoughts came back to Falcon. No matter how hard he focused on work, the moment idle thoughts crept in, they led back to his new boyfriend. It was probably normal, not even a week into dating, but for an otherwise logical man, it was sort of surprising.

Luckily, or unluckily, he had a distraction now. As he and Gregory found seats in the administration room, they were shortly joined by the other vets and vet techs. Nobody seemed to know what was going on, judging by the worried and puzzled expressions.

"Thanks for turning up," Dianne addressed them when everyone was there. "I hate to do this out of the blue, but circumstances have come up. We need to schedule some weekend training within the next month—mandatory—to review care standards."

That was like dropping a bomb of accusation in the middle of the room. Murmurs and exclamations swept the room.

"*Not* because I think anything is going wrong," Dianne added quickly. "I won't say it's routine, but we should also be prepared for inspections this week. Someone's dropped a word in the ear of the state humane society that... well. I won't repeat gossip, but certain individuals seem to think we're not up to scratch here."

"Fuck that," Gregory said, rising to his feet. For once, it was Blane pulling him down and squeezing his arm to remind him that he was in the workplace. "I mean... sorry, but that is ridiculous. We get dragged over the coals for doing our jobs like always?"

"It's not my call," Dianne told him solemnly. "I have your backs. But there's a food chain, and I'm not at the top."

Jolene, one of the vet techs, crossed her arms and glared at the floor. "I just went through my continuing education modules."

"I know. It's going to be inconvenient, but we have got to prove that we go above and beyond like we all know we do." Dianne sighed. "The more proof I have—education credits," she gestured toward Jolene, "and satisfactory inspections, and so on, the better."

They didn't know anything more by the end of the meeting. All they established was that Dianne wasn't budging on the recertification requirements, and she wasn't saying who had the problem. If it was someone from another zoo, or the state inspector, it would be much more important, as far as Blane was concerned. Some random administrator? He didn't care. *He* knew he did the best job he could.

He shut it off for the afternoon as he went about work, pouring his attention into helping Gregory safely tranquilize one of the giraffes so they could x-ray her leg and diagnose her ongoing limp. It was grueling work at times, but better than working in private practice lifting eighty-pound German Shepherds onto operating tables unassisted.

By the end of the day, though, he and Gregory were sweaty and exhausted.

"Oh, God. I have a date, too," Blane remembered as he washed up.

Gregory laughed. "Hope you brought a change of clothes."

"Of course." Blane always did, but those clothes had become a little fancier since seeing Falcon. Collared shirts instead of t-shirts, say. Not *too* over-the-top. But he still smiled as he did up the buttons.

"Well, who knows what all that was about?" Gregory grabbed his jacket and car keys. "What are we gonna do?"

"Carry on like always," Blane shrugged. It was obvious to him. "If anyone has a problem, they'll bring it up with me. But you and I know we do our damn jobs."

Gregory slowly relaxed. "Yeah. Yeah, you're right. All right. Catch you later. Have fun tonight."

"I will," Blane promised. He deserved that much after today.

"How was your day?"

It was the question Blane had been preparing for on the short drive over to the little Italian place he and Falcon had agreed upon.

"Oh, a lot happened, but nothing worth writing home about," Blane answered, dodging rather than lying. He didn't let his personal life bleed into his work with the animals; he sure as hell wasn't going to ruin the mood and let his work stress bleed into his personal life, either.

Falcon furrowed his brows. "Sounds… intriguing."

"Not really," Blane laughed. "You?"

"Oh, I heard from my sister's friend and we finalized the contract for the commissions."

"*That's* exciting!" Blane exclaimed. "Who would have thought?"

"I know. Apparently the guy's wife just adores them. Some people are obsessed with pandas, some people love dolphins…" Falcon laughed.

Blane chuckled. "And some people like naked mole-rats, I'm sure."

Falcon nearly spat his ice water. "Hardly appropriate conversation for dinner."

"It's not the fanciest Italian place in Knoxville. Man, that's an oxymoron."

Falcon leaned in. "Any place with you is fancy."

"I'm not sure you would have said that a couple hours ago while I was trying to get a giraffe's leg up." Blane grinned as Falcon laughed. "But thanks anyway."

"You're in a good mood," Falcon commented.

Faking it 'til I make it. "I do my best," Blane answered. "Garlic bread? If I get it, we have to share."

Falcon laughed again. "That feels like a deal with the devil." He looked happy, though, as he closed the menu. "When are we meeting up with your friends again?"

It was the second or third time he'd brought it up since the weekend, and Blane was beginning to suspect a case of nerves. He smiled gently. "Saturday." *Assuming the training isn't this weekend.* "Why?"

"Just checking." Falcon opened the menu again and flipped it shut, fidgeting with the pages.

Before Blane could ask any more questions, the waiter arrived to take their orders. By the time he was gone, it felt weird to pursue the subject, and Falcon was talking again anyway.

"We should make this a regular thing. Choose a different restaurant and go there, sometime during the week. It'll break up your work week and… well, the days of the week aren't real for me, but sort of mine, too," he laughed.

"Yeah. That sounds nice." Blane gazed at Falcon. "You know, I was worried about this stage. The early dating stage."

Falcon propped his chin on his fist. "Why?"

"Worried about not knowing what to do. Arranging everything, figuring out how often we should see each other…"

Falcon leaned in. "Nothing has to change because we put a label on it. We can keep going on dates a few times a week, staying over sometimes, like before."

Blane nodded slowly. He had a point there. "I guess that makes sense. God, I feel like I'm a teen again, trying to figure out how all this works."

"How do you think I feel?" Falcon laughed, fiddling with his utensils. "I've never had a boyfriend in public. And now…"

Blane reached over the table to touch Falcon's hand, and left his hand there. "I'm happy to show you off."

"And to let me in," Falcon murmured, his gaze flickering up to Blane's face.

Blane tried to remain inscrutable as he nodded. "That, too, I guess."

"My grumpy little vet," Falcon added with a teasing wink.

Blane scoffed. "Here comes the garlic bread. We'll see if you want to get cozy after that."

"Always," Falcon winked, and Blane's heart lifted.

Everything will sort itself out, somehow. I can believe that when I'm with him.

CHAPTER

<h1 style="text-align:center">Twenty-Five</h1>

FALCON

A BURST OF LAUGHTER AND NOISE GREETED THEM AS SOON AS Falcon pushed open the bar door and stepped inside the darkened bar. He had no idea who he was looking for, but he looked around anyway.

"There they are. Let's meet them."

Well, at least they weren't dragging out the inevitable. Falcon looked over the table of beefy men, two of whom were jostling each other, and gulped. "Sure."

"Don't be nervous. They'll love you," Blane assured him, putting his arm around Falcon's shoulders to lead him up to the table.

"Awww, look at the lovebirds!" one of the guys exclaimed when they were close by, to a round of laughter.

Roman was there—Falcon knew him, at least. He offered a quick, grateful smile for his presence. "Hey."

"Hi again. Didn't bring your cute friend for me?" Roman's lips pulled down in a mock-sad face. "I'm not sure you can sit with us."

"*Tell me* that was a Mean Girls reference." Falcon had

hardly noticed the slender guy in the suit, sitting quietly in the corner, until he spoke up.

"It… I plead the fifth. I don't have that much choice of English-language movies sometimes," Roman protested.

Blane laughed, his arm still around Falcon's shoulder. "Guys, this is Falcon. You already know Roman."

Falcon tried to keep up with the names of the rest of them: Nico and Deen were a couple, judging by the lack of personal space between them. But Josh kept casting wide-eyed looks at Deen in particular, which was a little confusing. Tyler was already several beers in and beaming at everyone like they were his new best friend. Finally, Dustin was the scrawnier guy, especially in comparison to the rest of them, but he suited the suit well.

"Right. Uh. I'll definitely remember that," Falcon laughed sheepishly as everyone scooted their chairs around to make room for the two of them.

"Beers all around?" Blane was off to the bar before Falcon could follow, leaving him alone with the guys.

"You're an artist, right?" Josh leaned in across the table. "What's with all the creatives lately?"

"Hey. I'm not the new guy anymore. Knock that off," Deen told him and flipped him off.

Josh got flustered for a moment before laughing.

Something about Deen looked familiar, and it only clicked the moment Deen added, "I'm a musician."

"Oh. Shit. Deen… Jayse?" Falcon tried, suddenly realizing why Josh had looked starstruck. "Sorry, I don't listen to modern music, but…" *Of course I know the name.*

"Yeah." Deen was carefully casual, like he was trying not to attract attention. That was probably exactly it, too.

So Falcon matched his tone to play it cool. "Nice to meet you. You and Nico…?"

"He's my boyfriend," Nico nodded. "Hence why he's the newest to the group, before you."

"Uh oh," Falcon laughed. Hearing that he and Blane weren't the token gay couple made him relax immediately. He glanced around at them, trying to read them. His gaydar was definitely going off, but he didn't want to outright ask.

"Did he not say? We're all gay," Roman laughed. "Or bi," he added after a moment. "You know. Generally into dudes."

Falcon laughed. "No, he didn't." Instantly his guard was lower. "Cool. Is that how you met?"

"More or less. We all met in school," Blane said, sidling up behind Falcon to pass out beers before taking a seat next to him. "And now here we are."

"Pretending to be adults," Josh snorted.

"Well, *some* of us are dating like it," Nico added with a smug smirk, which earned him a glare from Roman and rolled eyes from Josh.

"Look at him. Gets a boyfriend—after, what, six years of celibacy? And now he's too good for us," Roman groaned.

"*Hey*," Nico protested, but Deen was laughing. "Et tu?"

"Sorry, babe." Deen cleared his throat and tried for a reproachful gaze at Roman.

Falcon laughed, leaning into Blane when his boyfriend's shoulder pressed against his. This definitely felt like acceptance already.

"We'll have to hold a contest." Dustin's lips quirked mischievously. "Last one left single…"

"Gets a Grindr profile made for him? By us?" Blane grinned wickedly. "I'd love to watch that."

Roman gasped. "Oh, dude. That's not fair. Some of us have jobs."

"Yeah," Tyler grumbled. "Which require travel. All of us, in fact."

Nico and Blane exchanged looks. "Excuses," Nico said. "All I hear is excuses."

"Maybe we don't *want* boyfriends," Roman added.

That earned him a skeptical look from every other person at the table, and Falcon stifled his laughter. Even *he* had the inkling Roman wasn't as much a playboy as he made himself out to be.

"*Anyway*," Josh said pointedly. "I need a few more beers in me before I'll agree to any more bullshit dares."

"I seem to remember you being the first on board every time a stupid dare comes up, actually," Tyler said thoughtfully. "But yeah, let's move on to the next round of mocking. Who wants to share life updates?"

Falcon bit back his smile and looked around the table.

Josh shrugged. "Sure, me first. Absolutely nothing. Except dumbass tourists, and a barn-raising for one of my neighbors."

"A *barn-raising*? Like, frontier-style?" Dustin looked fascinated. "Little House on the Prairie?"

"Yeah. Nerd," Josh added in a mumble. When Dustin reached for his arm, he jerked away and held his hands up like Dustin was threatening him, while the others chuckled. "I didn't say anything!"

Dustin eyed him. "Sure you didn't. Nothing new here, either. My boss congratulated me on something not long ago, but I shouldn't talk about it yet."

"Busting crime and saving the world?" Blane smiled proudly. "That's our boy."

Dustin looked embarrassed at the attention and waved it off, ducking his head and draining his nearly-finished beer instead.

"I guess me next," Blane shrugged. "*This* is pretty new," he beamed, shaking Falcon's shoulder lightly.

"Cheers to that." They all leaned in to clink beer bottles, and Falcon felt his cheeks flush with pleasure.

"Then there's the usual work bullshit," Blane added, almost as an afterthought. He looked pointedly at Roman. "And you?"

The usual work bullshit? Falcon eyed his boyfriend, but Blane wasn't looking at him. Blane hadn't mentioned anything in the last couple weeks out of the ordinary, but he had seemed a little weird the other night at the Italian place.

Roman frowned, but he didn't push Blane. Instead, he announced, "I'm no longer the new guy. I should be on a pretty consistent route now."

It seemed to be a night for celebration, because Nico and Deen announced they were moving in together part-time—as soon as Nico's current schedule month came to an end. They were aiming for Nico to move to another role in the National Park Service by Christmas, so they could live together full-time for real.

"Well, compared to that, I got nothing," Tyler shrugged broadly, and everyone laughed. "Uh, I shaved a couple seconds off my qualifying time in practice? Ain't shit until it's official though."

"Athletics?" Falcon asked.

"Racecars."

Falcon perked up. "Oh! Awesome." He knew nothing about them, but it sounded badass.

Their beers were almost gone, so Blane rose to his feet.

"Nuh uh. My round," Roman told him and got up, too.

"Fine. I'll help carry them."

"I can help," Falcon offered, but Blane shook his head.

"I've got it."

He watched them head off. Their expressions were more serious now as they leaned together at the bar. Blane was leaning in to talk to Roman when Nico's voice interrupted Falcon's reverie.

"So, I hear there was some kind of wedding?"

"Oh. Yeah. My sister's." Falcon dragged his gaze away from the two of them. "That was cool, as weddings go. I got a sweet boyfriend out of it, so…"

"Not a lot of weddings have that perk," Josh laughed in his slow drawl.

Nico grinned. "There's your problem. Go to more weddings."

Josh spoke vehemently after a second of contemplation. "Uh… hmm, let's see. No. I get enough goddamn honeymooners at the ranch."

"Oh, you run one?"

Josh gave a long-suffering sigh. "The tourist trap kind, yep. If you've ever wanted the sanitized version of a farm experience, I've got just the place."

Falcon laughed. "I'll keep that in mind. I could use references for horses. Their anatomy is… tricky."

"Oh, yes," Josh agreed. "Sure is."

Blane and Roman were back with beers, and Falcon was almost able to let go of the little moments of weirdness.

Almost.

He wasn't so drunk he couldn't pay attention to where the taxi was going. The two of them were heading back to Blane's place, since it was bigger. And Blane had had the same number of beers as Falcon.

Which meant they weren't too drunk to talk about this. In fact, Falcon hoped the beer would loosen his tongue.

"So, you said earlier," he said to attract Blane's attention. "Work bullshit."

Blane winced and looked at him, which definitely meant something was up. "I… Yeah. It's not a big deal. I didn't want you worrying."

Falcon eyed him. "You know now I'll be worrying more, right? You remember how long we managed to *not* get together because we didn't talk about it?"

"Ah." Blane sheepishly laughed. "Yeah."

"I saw you talking to Roman about it. I won't push if you don't wanna say," Falcon said slowly. "But I do want to support you."

Blane took his hand and squeezed, rubbing it lightly in the darkness of the backseat of the taxi. Falcon's eyes flickered to the front, but Blane didn't seem worried, so he looked back at him. "Thank you. Sorry I didn't say. I just don't know much yet, you know?"

Falcon nodded silently and waited.

"The bosses are… agitating. They want us to go through retraining for humane certifications, they wanna check vet records, that kind of stuff. Inspections."

"What? Why? Was there an incident?" Falcon frowned. He couldn't picture Gregory or any of the keepers he'd met mistreating an animal.

"No, that's the thing. Someone anonymous complained or something, I think. We don't know why the bosses are taking it seriously. I mean, we get animal rights protestors who think *any* confinement—even animals who can't be released into the wild—is wrong. They know to ignore them."

"So what's different here?" Falcon murmured.

Blane's expression was stormy. "I have an idea."

But even though Falcon prompted him, Blane wouldn't say. Falcon eventually let it drop, with just a promise from Blane to tell him what happened when everything shook out next week.

Tumbling into bed with Blane half an hour later, Falcon felt him tossing and turning for a few minutes before sleep finally claimed him. It was clearly worry, which wasn't like him.

In turn, Falcon stayed awake for a few more minutes, worrying and thinking about everything Blane had said until sleep finally pulled him into its grasp.

Twenty~Six

BLANE

DDIANNE'S HANDWRITING WAS NOT UNFAMILIAR, BUT IT SURE was unwelcome. There was a note from her in Blane's locker when he got to work on Monday morning, and he didn't like the sound of it at all.

Can you come see me in the admin building this morning? —Dianne.

It made no sense to dwell on the worst possible outcome, but Blane still thought it: what the hell would he do if he lost his job? Positions like his didn't open frequently in zoos.

"Hey, man." Gregory was dressed for business and looked like he meant it. "Ready to fight the weekend sniffles?"

"Why, what's going on?"

"One of the keepers was telling me there's something going around the monkey exhibits."

"Oh, great," Blane sighed. "No, I gotta run and see Dianne first."

Gregory stopped halfway to the door. "About...?" He sounded wary.

"Hell if I know."

"All right. Come as soon as you can. I should be able to get things started."

"Yep. See you soon," Blane told Gregory, his chest tight. There was no reason he should be worried, but fuck it, now he was.

On his way to the office, Blane took a minute to mentally review everything he'd done last week. He couldn't think of a single issue, or even something he could have handled differently. If this was about the way they'd tranquilized their giraffe, well, they followed every damn procedure every time...

He pushed open the office door and knocked, then let himself in.

"Come in, sit down. Thanks for coming," Dianne told him, rising to his feet to greet him before she sat again.

"Hi. Of course. What's up? Is something wrong?"

"Oh, no. No," Dianne told him, but it didn't reassure him. "It's about the art program."

It took Blane a few seconds to realize what she meant: the animals' art enrichment for the auctions. That was starting today, this afternoon, if their schedule allowed. He'd been looking forward to Falcon visiting later today to watch. "Oh?"

"We might have to put that on hold for a week or two. I've spoken to the fundraising and marketing teams about it —they said it will be a few months until the next auction anyway."

"Whoa, wait." Blane sat up straight. "Do you mean not doing the art with them at all? The meerkats were gonna be tomorrow, and the elephants later this week."

"That's what I mean."

"Why? Don't tell me someone said it's animal cruelty,

because if someone's been reading up on the internet..." Blane trailed off, narrowing his eyes.

"Oh, we know it isn't." Dianne drummed her fingers against the keyboard. "Some things have been... published about the zoo on the internet."

"What do you mean?"

Dianne typed for a few moments, then turned her screen toward him.

Blane leaned in to look at the zoo's Google review average: two-point-something stars. The same on Yelp, and Trip-Advisor.

He reeled. "Aren't we... I mean, I don't Google us all the time, but..."

"Our average has consistently been much higher," Dianne agreed grimly. "Until last week, when a campaign of one-stars was begun against us. Now there are people from far away on the internet leaving one-star reviews, supposedly from a wide date range, complaining about all sorts of unrelated things. Upkeep, animal care, signage—hell, even parking."

"It can't be a competitor," Blane shook his head. Not even the shitty for-profit zoos that were barely more than animal prisons engaged in that kind of behavior.

"We don't know. My bosses have been trying to get in touch with these websites to see what can be done. But it's been carefully arranged. These are all different accounts and such."

Blane went cold. "When exactly did it start?"

"It's hard to tell, but we think sometime mid-last week."

No way. He had to get proof before he said anything. "I'm gonna look that up later and see what I can find out. But this is seriously... I mean, the animals enjoy it. It's enrichment."

Dianne frowned. "I know."

No, you don't get it. This isn't just one-star reviews. Taking away any activity narrows my animals' whole world. But he couldn't argue with his boss, so Blane clenched his jaw tightly and nodded.

"I'll talk with them some more and see what we can do. And, Blane? There's one more thing."

* * *

If it weren't for his habit of stopping in front of the door of the clinic and taking a few deep breaths, letting all his personal stress and tension go, Blane would have burst inside.

As it was, he walked slowly, but he found it hard to compartmentalize that rage.

Gregory was leaning over a notepad, making notes. He glanced at Blane, then did a double-take and looked around to see if they were alone. For now, they were. "What's up? You look like you wanna punch something."

"What's next?" Blane countered. He wasn't going to get wound up before he worked with an animal.

"I'm going out for a look at the monkeys. You stick here and fill prescriptions," Gregory told him. "Did it go okay?"

"No painting with the animals this week."

"No shit. Why?"

"Someone's leaving fake one-star reviews on the zoo online, and they're trying to… I dunno. Clean up our image. I guess this is preventative, so people can't go all, *ooh, they must be torturing the elephants into painting.*" Blane bit back his anger. "No, those are the assholes in the circuses and shit. Which is why our elephants' paintings are abstract."

"Whoa. Deep breath." Gregory cracked a smile. "Don't make me break out the tranqs."

Blane managed a smile in return and breathed in and out for a count of four until he relaxed again. "I think it's my boyfriend's ex. It started last week, after he got kicked out of the wedding. And something else she said… made me suspect."

Gregory nodded slowly. "Have you found him behind it yet?"

"Not yet, but you know what I'm spending my lunch break doing."

"Right there with you." Gregory clapped his arm. "I gotta go check out our little buddies. You all right?"

Blane nodded. He couldn't let the jerk get him into trouble, after all. He had to play the long game. "I'll be good. We have plenty to do today to keep me busy anyway."

Which reminded him to send a text to Falcon and tell him not to bother coming in today.

He couldn't wait for tonight to take that asshole down.

Twenty-Seven

FALCON

Don't bother coming in today. TTYL.

It was by far the bluntest text Falcon had gotten from Blane at work, but to be fair, it was also sent around 9:30—not during his lunch hour, when they often chatted about how their days were going.

Nothing about the situation put Falcon at ease. He tried sending a text back.

What's going on? Call me at lunch?

But lunchtime came and went—even the late lunch Blane usually took after food prep—and he had no word from Blane.

Falcon tried to distract himself with work, but it was no use. Backgrounds were about the most intensive thing he could bring himself to paint today, and even that took focus.

He tried another text after lunch: *Want to meet after work?*

Still no answer. Falcon's mind went to the worst: he'd been fired. He was sick. Something horrible had happened at the zoo. He searched news headlines, but found nothing.

Until he clicked back in the search results and something

caught his eye—the review page for the zoo, with a way lower average than he'd expected.

Curious about what on earth anyone could find wrong with the place, he clicked. Sure, it was a bit shabby, but they put their money into animal welfare, not new signs and gourmet restaurants.

"What the hell?"

The last five reviews were all one or two stars—no, more than that. He quickly scanned them, eyes narrowing. All left within the last week or so, and all mentioning different combinations of things: zoo upkeep, animal welfare, you name it.

Falcon narrowed his eyes. This would explain why upper management was getting touchy. Did Blane know yet? He couldn't very well tell him by text message.

I'm coming to pick you up from work. Be there at 5, he texted Blane.

He reached the parking lot a few minutes early to find a spot, then waited by Blane's car again.

Falcon still had no answer as five o'clock came and went, but the unmistakable rolling gait of the man approaching caught his attention.

He could practically see the storm clouds around Blane's head, and it took him a dizzying moment to resist the urge to run.

It's Blane. I'm okay. He's not angry at me, he reminded himself, chewing his nail.

Blane looked startled and stopped for a second, then raised a hand to wave and walked faster toward the car. "Hon? What are you doing here?"

"I texted you."

Blane frowned. "Sorry. My phone died. I was pretty intensively… Googling stuff over lunch."

"Pizza," Falcon said firmly. "You and me. We have to talk about this."

Blane swallowed but nodded. "Yeah, we do."

He dropped his stuff off in the car, and then Falcon led him toward his own ride.

Pizza would help. It had to help.

<hr>

Once their order was delivered to the car, Falcon rolled up his window, opened the pizza box, and turned to Blane. "I Googled the zoo."

Blane let out a slow sigh and shook his head. "Shit. Okay. You found the reviews?"

"Yeah. Did you know about them?" Falcon tore the lid off the pizza box and handed it over.

"Not until today." Blane took a couple slices, then shifted in his seat to face him better, drawing a leg up under himself. "And there's more. Did you look at the reviews?"

"Yeah, some of them. A lot of bullshit."

"There's a review complaining about me. It's not like *all* the reviews do. Just one, so it looks innocuous."

It hit Falcon like a ton of bricks. He sat up fast, almost dumping the pizza box off his lap and onto the floor. "Shit," he hissed, catching it, but his thumb went into the melted cheese and steaming hot crust. "Fuck!"

Blane leaned over to grab his hand and pull it into his lap, then calmly took the lid off his cup of water and guided Falcon's thumb into it.

"Oof," Falcon grunted as cold water hit tingling skin, but

the relief was almost immediate. "Goddamn, their pizzas are hot."

"Yeah, but it shouldn't be serious," Blane told him. "Just keep it in there for a minute." His hand was still on Falcon's.

Falcon offered a little smile. "How the fuck can anyone say you're less than professional when... *that* happened?"

Blane's expression darkened instead of cleared. "Because it's Spencer."

"Yeah. I just figured that out," Falcon admitted. "Do you know for sure?"

"I can't tell for sure, no. But I sure as hell plan to find out," Blane told him, finally letting go of his hand. "How's that?"

Falcon drew his thumb out and flexed it, then nodded. Just a little sting. "I'll be fine. Thanks, hon."

"Anytime," Blane said, finally relaxing out of the cool, collected medical professional mode. He blew on a pizza slice and started eating while Falcon did the same.

After a few minutes, Falcon shook his head. "But you knew something was going on before? Did you suspect it was him?"

"Yeah. I kind of had an inkling. The timing..."

"Tell me," Falcon urged him, setting down his pizza slice. "We can't do this if we keep secrets."

Blane hesitated and worked his way through a pizza slice, and Falcon gave him a minute to compose his thoughts. Finally, Blane said, "I thought hearing about him might upset you."

"No," Falcon shook his head firmly. "Besides, why not get me involved? I'm the only person who can talk sense into him."

"No. Absolutely not." Blane reached out for Falcon's hand again, but this time, he squeezed. "That's what he *wants*."

Now that he put it that way, Falcon could see his point. "Oh. Shit, yeah. I thought it was just, like, a revenge thing."

Blane shook his head. "I wouldn't trust the creepy git for a second."

"Me neither. So what do we do?"

"Well, for starters, I keep my head down at work and do everything perfectly, because they're gonna be watching me the closest," Blane muttered. "Asshole."

"What did they say?"

"That I act unprofessional with the animals. Too familiar with them. I don't know. Dianne said, but I was… well, trying not to lose my cool."

Falcon sat up straight. "Okay, this is going to sound creepy, but bear with me."

Blane raised a brow.

Falcon fought the blush and cleared his throat, taking a deep drink before he spoke again. "So, uh, I had to take a bunch of photo references with animals. And a lot of them have you in them."

After a second of staring at him, Blane started to crack a smile. "You were stalking me."

"Was not."

"Totally were," Blane laughed. "Taking photos of me at work?"

"I… wanted you in the background of some of my paintings," Falcon muttered, avoiding Blane's gaze.

But Blane took his hand again. "God knows I'm not complaining. If you're saying what I think you're saying, you might just be about to save my neck."

"Yeah?" Falcon looked up at Blane. "Think it would work?"

"I think we have to tell them everything."

Falcon winced, but he nodded. "I'll come in with you tomorrow, if that'll help. Or tonight. Whatever you need."

Blane squeezed his hand for a long moment before letting go. "And that's why I love you."

"Love you too," Falcon murmured with a smile.

"Love to take photos of me at work and study them when I'm not around, more like…"

"Oh, God." Falcon rolled his head back against the seat. "I'm never gonna hear the end of this."

"Nope," Blane cheerily told him. Already, his mood was so much brighter than when he'd walked up to him in the parking lot, and it made Falcon smile regardless of the teasing.

"How much do I bribe you for your silence to your friends? And mine? Oscar would *lose* it," Falcon groaned.

"I don't know if there's any amount that will work," Blane told him. "I think I can get years of mileage out of this."

Years? When Falcon looked over at Blane, the expression on his face—love, gratitude, hope—made his heart melt.

"Years," he repeated in a murmur. "Now eat up."

Twenty~Eight

BLANE

"I can't apologize enough for bringing all of this into work."

Beside him, Blane felt Falcon wince. He knew his boyfriend was blaming himself, as much as he'd reassured him all last night that it was not his fault.

"No, I appreciate that you're being upfront. You said you had something to tell me about this whole issue?" Dianne looked curiously between the two of them.

"Okay. This is my new boyfriend, Falcon. Falcon, Dianne, my boss here."

Dianne looked startled for a moment, and Blane resisted the urge to physically cross his fingers that he hadn't made a grave miscalculation. Then, she nodded. "Let me guess. The review about you specifically… or the whole campaign? Is this a homophobic thing?"

Blane blinked. "Um—"

"Yes, ma'am," Falcon cut in. He cleared his throat. "It's also a jealousy thing. Closeted self-loathing stereotypes, you know. I think he orchestrated the campaign, and I know for sure he targeted Blane."

"Got it." Dianne cracked her knuckles and rolled her shoulders, her face splitting into a smile. "Thank you for coming to me. I *know* I can get the leverage I need to take down those reviews. I'm going to tell them you're considering opening a police investigation. Are you?"

"Yeah," Falcon said, which surprised Blane even more. Blane turned quickly to look at him, but his face was steely and resolute. "If he doesn't leave me alone—and now Blane, and everyone employed here."

"Okay." Dianne leaned in. "I know it's hard in this part of the country, but there's a lot of us who have your back. Jealous ex, random internet troll, I don't care. We take our employees' side."

Blane's chest grew tight with emotion. He'd never directly come out to Dianne before. Not that he'd avoided it, but it hadn't come up.

Kind of like Falcon, actually, when he thought about it.

"I really appreciate it," he said quietly. "I know this is a hell of a mess to sort out."

"It's not your fault," Dianne said firmly, and at last, it actually started to sink in. Blane had spent so long saying that to Falcon that a part of him had started to feel like it was *his* fault, if anyone's.

But she was right. It was Spencer being... well, from the sounds of it, Spencer.

"The other reason I'm here," Falcon spoke up, reaching out to squeeze Blane's hand and bring him back to Earth, "is because I have photos of Blane at work. I'm an artist. I've been getting references of your animals for the past few months, and a lot of them have him in them. I took all the ones I could find." He handed a USB stick over the desk and leaned back. "If it's any help at all, that's everything I could find. I have some photos of the animal enrichment programs, too, since some of the reviews were talking about the animals being bored and cooped up and that kind of stuff."

"That's a tremendous help," Dianne said and offered him a smile. "Bright guy you've got here," she added to Blane.

Blane flushed with pleasure and squeezed Falcon's hand in return. "Thank you, ma'am. He is."

Falcon looked embarrassed and waved it off. "It just upset me. I've been watching everyone at work for the last month, and… yeah. All those lying reviews. And I was worried about Blane in particular, but nobody here deserves that kind of garbage."

"Are you prepared to bring it to the press if this gets ugly?" Dianne asked them both.

Blane looked at Falcon, then back at her. "Actually… I think we'd need to talk about that."

"I would if you would," Falcon told him. "Whatever you think is best for you and the zoo."

"You only just—to your family—and your job?" Blane didn't know how many people in Falcon's line of work knew about him. Surely he'd come out to them before, but maybe not.

"Everyone important to me knows," Falcon told him and looked back at Dianne. "If it will help, or get you positive press, and if Blane's okay with it, I leave the decision to you guys. It *is* kind of my fault everyone else got dragged into this. So yeah, I'll go to the police if it'll get the review sites to take that stuff down. Or the press. Whatever helps."

Blane let a breath escape as he watched Falcon. *I'm so damn lucky.* "You don't have to."

"I want to. It's the right thing to do," Falcon said firmly.

Dianne nodded. "Okay. Falcon, thank you for meeting me and telling me everything. Blane, I'll talk to you later today, okay? I have to call my bosses and fill them in, and see what we can get done with this new information."

They both shook hands, and then they were outside, still holding hands.

Blane felt stunned at everything that had just unfolded. "I think I'm off the chopping block."

"Well, they know it's all groundless bullshit rumors now," Falcon told him. "You okay?"

After the last week of stress and vague threats, Blane had never felt better. "I—yeah. Really okay. Way better."

"Oh, and Blane?" Dianne stood in the doorway, shielding her eyes against the morning sun.

Blane automatically straightened up and answered, "Yes, ma'am?"

"The animal art program can go ahead. I don't care what my bosses say—you and the keepers have all told me it enriches the animals' lives. Falcon, I know you were approved to help out with it, following the relevant handling procedures, of course. It would be a great pleasure to have you here."

Falcon looked like he might be about to cry, but he beamed brightly in return. "Thank you, ma'am."

It would take Blane a day or two to arrange a new schedule with the keepers, but he relished the prospect of letting Falcon get a little closer to the animals—not enough to handle them, of course, or get in the way, but a behind-the-scenes look that few people got to experience.

"That's awesome," Blane murmured once they were alone

again, wandering toward the front gate with his boyfriend. "Are you gonna hang out here for the day?"

"I was gonna work today, but you know what? I think I'll stick around," Falcon said with a playful smile. "And tonight, pizza date."

"Is pizza our food now?"

"Sure is," Falcon grinned. Gregory was approaching, so Falcon let go of his hand. "I'll let you get to work now."

"I don't think we've been really introduced." Gregory grinned at them both. "Is this the guy you won't shut up about?"

Falcon was looking at him with a teasing smile, and Blane felt the back of his neck and ears heat up. "It—yeah, this is him. Falcon. Gregory."

"How'd the meeting go?"

"Great," Blane told him, the relief rushing out in a sigh. "Just great. She supports us, and she's going to try to explain to the websites that it's a targeted homophobic harassment campaign."

"Sweet," Gregory exclaimed. "I mean, not that—you know. That they can do something."

Blane laughed. "Yeah, obviously. And I'm out of trouble, too. Falcon had a bunch of photos of me, and the enrichment programs day to day, that kind of stuff to back up their CCTV and inspections and whatever else they do."

"Seriously? Photos of him at work?" Gregory grinned.

Blane joined in his laugh. "I know! I was just teasing him last night—hey! Come back!" Falcon was pretending to stride away.

Falcon turned and sighed heavily at him. "You're such a jerk."

"I know."

"Ew. Young love. I'll be over there," Gregory waved toward the clinic and rolled his eyes. "Nice to meet you."

"You too," Falcon said with a chuckle. Then, he patted Blane's cheek. "Go on, get to work. I'll be here when you're done."

"And tonight, pizza."

"Pizza. And no secrets."

Blane had never poured so much feeling into a single word as when he said, "None."

CHAPTER
Twenty~Nine
FALCON

"Check it out! All the new reviews on Google are gone!"

Falcon wiped the paint off his hands and hurried to look over Blane's shoulder at his laptop. Just like Blane said, the reviews looked like they'd been reset. He beamed. "Fucking awesome. What about the others?"

"Still up," Blane admitted. "But I figured it wouldn't be this fast. Some of them might not do it, some might want evidence. Some review sites say they'll never delete reviews for any reason."

"Seriously?" Falcon stared at Blane. "Never?"

"Yep. God knows how long it'll take."

Falcon wrapped his arms around Blane's shoulders after checking himself for stray paint splatters. "That's amazing, though," he murmured. "Progress already."

"Are you done for the day?"

Blane had been so patient with him that Falcon couldn't resist. His work could wait until tomorrow. "Done," Falcon promised. "Let me wash up."

"Oooh, sexy."

"Not the mineral spirits part," Falcon laughed. "After the pre-cleanup, it could be. Or I could just clean up and then be ready for… anything." He breathed the last word into Blane's ear and nibbled his ear.

"Go," Blane told him firmly.

Falcon snickered. "Bossy." He pulled away and kissed Blane's cheek, then strode for the bathroom with his container of brushes. They always got rinsed before he did, so he never neglected to take care of them.

Then it was time to scrub his own self, which involved a quick shower since he'd managed to get spirits in his hair while cleaning, and get his hands and arms as clean as he could.

He wrapped a dry towel around his waist when he was finished, pushing his hair into some kind of order, and spun in the mirror to check himself out.

Time to go catch my man.

But first, he had one thing to do. Falcon dug his phone out from the pockets of his jeans, then dropped everything in the laundry basket. He leaned on the counter and opened up a text message to Spencer.

If all those fake reviews don't disappear by the end of the month, I'm taking it to the cops and letting Aunt Vera at you. Don't come near me or him or anyone I know ever again. Goodbye.

He hit *send* with a sense of determination, wishing the button actually clicked.

The message delivered, he blocked Spencer's number, then opened the bathroom door and sauntered out. He set his phone on the table as he passed, waiting until Blane looked up.

"Oh! Hello," Blane grinned, setting the laptop aside right away.

"Hi." Falcon sat sideways on Blane's lap and draped his arms around Blane's shoulders. "In the interests of not keeping secrets, I should tell you something."

Blane frowned and pecked his lips. "What's that?"

"I texted Spencer." Blane's eyes widened, but before he could answer, Falcon explained. "To tell him to get the other reviews taken down by the end of the month, or I'll go to the cops. I mean, chances are they won't do anything. Cyber-harassment isn't their specialty. But I know him, and he wants to avoid trouble. It might count as fighting dirty, but so does he."

"Look at you." Blane slid his arms around Falcon's waist and pulled him closer, pressing his lips in his damp hair. "I'm proud of you."

"And I blocked his number. Let him text a black hole forever," Falcon scoffed, rubbing his cheek against Blane's shoulder.

"Well, I have a secret, too. It's not a very well-kept one." Blane walked his fingers up Falcon's spine. "Seeing you half-dressed and clean makes me want to fix that."

A shiver of agreement ran down Falcon's spine. "I think you should show, not tell." He grinned at Blane.

The ground fell away from him as Blane scooped him into his arms and picked him up to carry him to the bed.

Falcon laughed and kept his arms around Blane's neck, even as his heart raced. "You can't resist showing off, can you?"

"I told you I want to show you off forever."

Falcon sank into the bed and beamed up at him. "You know how to flatter a guy."

"I know how to do a lot to a guy," Blane countered, tugging the towel away from his waist. "For example, unwrapping him like a present."

"Well, you have too much packaging," Falcon told him. "Don't you know it's bad for your environment?"

"My apologies," Blane laughed and stripped his t-shirt off. "Better?"

Falcon rocked his hand from side to side in a so-so motion. "Getting there."

"So demanding."

Once Blane was naked, Falcon ran his hands slowly up his boyfriend's chest, enjoying the smooth skin under his palms. "Much better."

Blane's forearms pressed against the bed on either side of his head as he swooped down to crush Falcon's lips in kiss after kiss, stealing his breath.

Falcon melted and let him press their lips together, flicking his tongue out in answer to Blane's. He dug his nails into Blane's back and scratched lightly, then rolled his head back so Blane could kiss at his throat and lip his earlobes.

"I love having a boyfriend who knows the spots I like."

Blane's voice was warm and growly and close to his ear. "I love having a boyfriend who's so damn fun to play with."

Falcon bit back his whimper and raised his hands above his head. "You've got me. Play to your heart's content."

Blane licked a slow trail down the center of his body, straight for his dick. One broad hand closed around Falcon's wrists while he kissed along the shaft.

The warm, wet suction against the outside of sensitive skin made Falcon squirm. The electric tingles of need were already building deep within him, and he wasn't sure he had the patience for whatever the hell Blane had in mind.

Blane let go of him and wrapped both hands around his cock, stroking one and then the other up his shaft in a continuous motion that felt too fucking good. Falcon moaned, rolling his head back into the bed and digging his nails into the bedspread. "Fuck!"

"You like that," Blane murmured, finally pausing his rhythm to lick the head of his now-throbbing hardness. Then he was sliding over smooth lips and onto Blane's tongue, the suction building around his head and down his shaft.

"Fuck, yeah, I do." Falcon swallowed and spread his legs, digging his heels into the bed.

Blane slowly pulled his head up, then pushed down again. He gradually sped up the rhythm, sucking Falcon's cock like a pro, and Falcon loved every second.

Especially when Blane paused and guided Falcon's hand to the back of his head.

"Oooh, *yeah*," Falcon approved, pushing up into Blane's mouth by arching his back, hips off the bed. He gently pushed the back of Blane's head, even his fingers tingling at the silky texture of Blane's hair between them.

After a minute of fucking those beautiful lips, Blane pulled his head away. "Not gonna let you come *that* fast."

"Aw," Falcon complained. "You'd better make up for it."

When Blane knelt upright, it was very clear how he intended to. His cock was hard now, pointing toward Falcon. Huge, flushed, and stiff, it was everything Falcon wanted in that second. Anticipation burned through him, and even Blane's slick fingers were nothing like what he wanted.

"You're so beautiful when you can't stop staring at my cock." Blane's voice was teasing, just enough to break through his reverie.

"Take the fucking compliment."

Blane chuckled deeply, the tone making Falcon forget the fullness of Blane's fingers inside him for a few moments. "Oh, I will. And anything else you wanna give me."

"Mmm," Falcon grinned. "Are you planning round two?"

"Can't be too prepared." Blane was rubbing his shaft now, and Falcon was sadly, achingly empty again.

For a very brief moment.

Blane never made him wait long before pushing into him, slow but steady. The extra lube made even the rounded head slide inside with ease.

"God, that's good," Falcon groaned as the burn made his toes curl, his fingertips tingling. His body was tight, so he took deep breaths to help Blane get every inch of that magnificence into him.

"I love how greedy you are for whatever you want," Blane whispered, moaning when he was all the way inside. "Oh, and how you feel. And the way you look at me. And your moans…"

"You just love me," Falcon beamed up at him. "Good thing I love you, too."

Blane chuckled and leaned down to press a kiss against Falcon's lips, his hand on Falcon's thigh. "Yeah. Damn good thing. Lie still, you cheeky bastard."

Falcon stopped squirming. "Fuck me, then," he breathed against Blane's lips, grinning as Blane's eyes darkened with lust.

Blane didn't waste a second getting into a rhythm. Slowly at first, then harder, he filled Falcon with every inch of him, Falcon's nerves sparking with pleasure at every thrust.

Falcon was squirming again, but he couldn't help himself; it felt too fucking good. His muscles twitched, stomach tight and fingers curled tightly as he rolled his head back. "Yes!"

Blane licked along his throat to his chin, then bent his head and sucked his nipple, his nails pressing into Falcon's thigh to keep him in place as he sank deep into him and joined their bodies.

The ecstasy flooding Falcon redoubled with every brush of Blane's skin against his, and every glimpse of the gorgeous, strong, compassionate man who had opened his heart to Falcon so quickly.

Whether he knows it or not, he's the one. Falcon would wait until Blane was ready to hear it, but part of him suspected he knew it, too. There was no mistaking the way they couldn't look away from each other when they made eye contact sometimes.

The future was for later, though. Right now, Falcon's thoughts were hazy and his body demanded all his brain-power. The fast, hard, deep staccato rhythm of Blane pushing against and into him was pushing him along so fast he could barely see straight.

"I'm gonna—too fast," Falcon gasped. He didn't want it to end. "Blane, you're gonna make me…"

"Come, baby," Blane growled. "I want to make you so happy. We have all fucking night together."

More than that, Falcon thought automatically. So long as they could remember what they'd already learned together, and they were willing to work for it, they had forever together.

He'd work his ass off to make Blane the happiest man alive, but just being here with him seemed to do the trick.

Falcon was pulsing already, shivering as the lightning-hot

crackles of need danced along his skin at every point where he brushed Blane's body.

The heat deep inside him couldn't be stopped a moment longer. He gasped and groaned Blane's name as he bucked against him and the world seemed to stop for a few precious seconds.

Hot and wet and sticky, he only started to come down before Blane was pushing erratically into him, his body slumping against Falcon's as quiet grunts of pleasure slipped from his throat.

Falcon rubbed his hands along Blane's back, his breath quickening as Blane left him wet and already aching for another round.

When Blane finally shifted off him to rest on his side, Falcon reached out to tangle his fingers lightly with his lover's.

"I love you," he whispered, tangling their legs together as they both caught their breath.

Blane's smile was soft and meant for him alone. "I love you, too."

Finally, it felt like he had the world within his grasp.

Epilogue

BLANE, THREE MONTHS LATER

Falcon's gasp was audible even from the next room of the airy home—airier still with less furniture than Blane would have liked.

But that would take time. Just reaching agreement on the wallpaper had taken long enough, and they'd both been impatient to move in and start their life together.

"What?" Blane prompted when Falcon didn't immediately say anything.

"Deen and Nico just got engaged!"

Blane stared. "Did they put it on Instagram?" As far as he knew, Falcon had just been checking his Instagram account —not Falcon's, the one Falcon had started for Blane. He'd insisted that hot vets were all the rage, and now he sneakily posted photos that Blane pretended not to know about.

And then Deen had gotten his fans on board somehow. Apparently Blane had a *following*.

He didn't really want to know about it. As far as he was concerned, as soon as the fake reviews had disappeared, he was done with the internet's opinion of him and his job.

"No, no. The group text. Dude. Check your phone once in a while," Falcon scoffed.

Blane smiled and joined Falcon in the former den, which they were turning into his main art space. He walked up behind him and grabbed his hips playfully. "I don't need to anymore. The guy I want to talk to is right here."

Falcon beamed up at him and tilted his head up to demand a kiss, so Blane obliged and leaned in to kiss him. "I bet we'll be getting a group phone call any minute now."

"The guys will want to go out for drinks, too. Any night work for you?"

Falcon hummed his agreement while Blane wrapped his arms around him. Blane supported him when he leaned back into him. "I'll make time any night," Falcon told him. "People don't just get engaged any day."

"They could," Blane murmured mischievously, watching Falcon's expression.

Falcon blushed, then grinned at him. "Is that a hint?"

"It might be. Is it a welcome hint?"

"Mmm. It might be. Don't let me beat you to the punch, that's all I'm saying," Falcon answered, winking.

Blane grinned. "One thing at a time, baby. We just got the house."

"I know. And there's something else… it's kind of your Christmas gift, but it's over Christmas." Falcon looked sheepish. "So I've been trying to figure out when to tell you."

Blane leaned in for a long, slow kiss, warmth igniting in his chest as their lips slid together.

Falcon finally pushed him playfully and handed over his phone. "You won't distract me that easily. Yet."

It took Blane a moment to realize what he was seeing: round-trip airline tickets. For two. To Paris. For Christmas.

He looked up sharply at Falcon. He'd only mentioned traveling to him once, but he'd remembered?

Of course he had.

Blane opened his mouth and then closed it again, clearing his throat, which was suddenly and strangely tight.

"Awww," Falcon murmured, turning around in his grip to take the phone back and hug him. "You like it?"

Blane shifted his hips so Falcon wouldn't press into his right thigh. His hand touched that pocket and the flat, but distinctive box within it. That could wait for a few weeks now.

"I love it. And you. No more stressing whose relatives to invite over for the first year, or... anything."

"We're still getting a tree," Falcon warned him, tapping his nose playfully. "Don't think you're escaping tree-hauling duties."

Blane laughed deeply. "For *that*, baby, I'll cut all the trees you want."

"Deforesting for me? How romantic." Falcon tucked his face into Blane's chest, and Blane hugged him tightly.

"Anything for you."

Slick

SIGNIFICANT BROTHERS #3

"NO STRINGS ATTACHED? GODDAMN, YOU BROUGHT A TOW ROPE."

Inches away from his dream of a leading role, catastrophe strikes for pro dancer Oscar. A friend of a friend offers a place to crash, and Oscar is grateful for the chance to rebuild his life. And when airline pilot Roman is at home, there's plenty of other benefits to enjoy…

The pair of them keep trying to get the steamy connection out of their system, but nothing works. Oscar only wants more—and it's clear that Roman feels the same. If only he could admit it.

As the fleet's youngest captain, Roman is growing tired of being Mr. Slick, partying in a new town every night. But he's an all-or-nothing kind of guy. When he tries commitment, he always overcommits and scares off boyfriends, ending up alone.

The last thing Roman expects is exactly what he's found in Oscar: a reason to come home.

As they chase an impossible dream, will these two free spirits break old habits… or each other's hearts?

About the Author

E. Davies writes feel-good, low-angst romance that never fades to black when the going gets good! Born in Canada, after 16 moves and counting, Ed has finally put down roots in north London.

He emerges from his writing nest to coo over fuzzy animals, flee from cute guys, dance through the streets with his chosen family, put together fierce looks, and—most of all—befriend local flowers.

You can find all available titles at: www.edaviesbooks.com

FOLLOW E. DAVIES ONLINE:

amazon.com/author/edavies
bookbub.com/authors/e-davies
facebook.com/edaviesauthor
goodreads.com/edavies
instagram.com/edaviesauthor
x.com/edaviesauthor

Also by E. Davies

Sunrise Island Brothers:

Collide

Stranded

Hart's Bay:

Hard Hart

Changed Hart

Wild Hart

Stolen Hart

Significant Brothers:

Splinter

Grasp

Slick

Trace

Clutch

Tremble

Riley Brothers:

Buzz

Clang

Swish

Crunch

Slam

Grind

Brooklyn Boys:

Electric Sunshine

Live Wire

Boiling Point

F-Word:

Flaunt

Freak

Faux

Forever

Freedom

After:

Afterburn

Afterglow

Aftermath

Shared Universes:

Shelter

Adore

Miracle

Redemption

Limelight

Barely Regal